A SAUCE STEALER

Margarita Meklina

SPUYTEN DUYVIL
New York City

Library of Congress Cataloging-in-Publication Data

Names: Meklina, Margarita, 1972-
Title: A sauce stealer / Margarita Meklina.
Description: New York City : Spuyten Duyvil, 2017.
Identifiers: LCCN 2017011308 | ISBN 9781944682507
Classification: LCC PG3549.M44 .A2 2017 | DDC 891.73/5--dc23
LC record available at https://lccn.loc.gov/2017011308

Black Line

1

First calculation, then calcium. Fetus and figures.

I figured out the day of my ovulation, measured temperature—and then strengthened my spine, spirit and stature with folic acid and calcium tablets in preparation, and calculated your due date.

Several days of elevated hopes and temperature had passed (you were already conceived) when I learned that your great grandfather had a grave form of cancer.

At ninety five, in a hospital bed, he was calling his *Yiddishe mommele* who had a wise look, a light complexion and the last name of Lightman, the one who luckily perished from illness in Byelorussia before the Nazis came to their place.

He lived through it all: waking up to hymns and hypocrisy on the radio, watching carefully prepared, crafty parades on TV, walking with fake and folksy factory workers waving Soviet flags.

Your great grandfather lived through all that and then, following his adventurous, adulterous kids, each with two wives (a live-in, right-in-your-face and a secret one "on-the-side," the one for whom business trips were invented), came to the U.S..

In California his skeptical self embraced Capitalism and capitulated to cancer.

That's what we assumed.

Stubborn and strong as he was, he could not be eradicated by extraneous forces (such as famine or fascists during World War II, or a freak accident later, when at ninety, on a cold rainy night, with a backpack on his shoulders, he was hit by a bus): with his outward strength toward the world, he could only be destroyed by himself, by his home-made cancerous cells.

And as soon as I knew that you'd live, I foresaw his impending imminent death.

Fetal movement or quickening, a manifestation of a quickly growing organism—and the fatal moment, the agony, disintegration.

That's—I foolishly thought—how life is.

2

And those butterflies... Your Italian father learned a new expression from me: butterflies in the stomach, a fragile feeling we both felt when we first met.

He strolled around an abandoned gas station with me, very serious in his suit (which, as I discovered later, he wore only a few times, favoring T-shirts of his beloved rock bands), and carried in his hand a cup with steamy espresso from a coffee house where we planted our blind date (the editor suggests "planned" but I'm talking about planting a seed of the date that in one month sprouted marriage). The cup was his protection: something to cling to, to clutch in his hand.

To get a hold of what was awaiting to happen. If we were in the nineteenth century which he, a history buff, dug, quoting the luminaries of that time with the same ease and elation as modern mammoths of history monographs, he probably would be tightening his grip on a rapier.

He was a large thirty-nine-year-old man, strikingly athletic and sturdy, with a Wild West streak sending him successively to all six continents, but weak in his heart, which started accelerating, legs walking slow and giving way, when he saw me. With his full yet not flabby calves and a pronounced, disproportionately large head, he reminded me of a gigantic infant.

Yes, he looked like a baby. And when a would-be baby in a womb moves, the sensation its mother experiences is sometimes referred to as "butterflies in the stomach." It's those tender taps of a thin yet stiff butterfly's wing against a womb's soft walls.

No wonder this story begins with a calculation—there is an arithmetic to life: at eleven gestational weeks, you were around three inches, at seventeen—six, but the quickening was supposed to start, according to a pregnancy book, when you scored eighteen-nineteen. Orchestrated by two skipped heartbeats (I came to a standstill sensing something unusual), it happened before: I felt you move when Yitzhak Perlman went on stage.

We did not surmise that somebody who played such empowering music could be so handicapped. Still, there was no contrast between his musical prowess and physical powerlessness (affected by polio, Perlman laboriously entered the stage relying on crutches). On the contrary, shiny steel "legs" seemed to give him more weight.

You did not move when he, purposely oblivious of the awestruck audience, casually walked to his chair. But right when the violin replied to his touch, I felt the butterflies.

The butterflies… they were there the day I first met your Italian father, and they reappeared, five years into our marriage, when you wanted to remind us of the beauty of love.

3

Linea nigra is a black line, a pigmented path, which runs from an expectant mother's navel to her pubic bone. When the line is undetected (and it is always undetected unless a woman is pregnant), they call it *linea alba*, a white line.

When an embryo is only a few days old, his future is outlined with invisible ink. When he grows, this concealed line—a conceived person's protruding presence—darkens and widens. A wavy green vine on a hospital monitor signifies a heartbeat; *linea nigra*, a black line—a blunt, blasphemous mother's triumph.

Look at somebody's grave: crisscrossed planks (or lines) are like a person's check-out from a hotel: he was here, and then a check mark was put in his place as though he left, deserted, escaped. Lines and arrows, bloody-red, on war maps show soldiers advancing; many will be shot dead.

Your great grandfather stored treacherous tracer bullets in his right shoulder: this triggered the interest of his grandkids. At our dacha in a subtle suburb of St. Petersburg (where a village would turn into a city without announcement), Granddad watered red puffed-up strawberries and green gaunt cucumbers, and we imagined him in his army fatigues and a green field cap with a red Soviet star. The hose in his muscular hands was like a machine gun.

Flesh flattens even before you succumb to the earth. Eyes become even, pale, teary lakes; cheeks are sunken. The body burrows into the sand, body tissue gives way and disappears, and what is left is a Zen line guarded by dusty digits on bare-boned granite: 1913—2007. And occasionally, you are an unknown hero soldier, and there is no trace at all.

We anticipated your great grandfather dying before you were born (one in and one out, as in an overcrowded warehouse), so we prematurely and erroneously erased him from our senses. He still engaged in conversations on conventional themes like his Medi-Cal or a medal given to him sixty years after the Nazis were crushed; he still cared about us and his contorted-by-illness-yet-continuing life, but his younger son said once, when a polyglot nurse, politely greeting us in Russian, English, and Spanish, turned on the TV for him: "He is already watching some other TV." As though there were some far away fantasies on phantom TVs available only to those who already had crossed a mysterious line.

What color is it when crossed? Is this transition to the other world indeed permanent, like a line drawn by a permanent marker?

For you, whose life is just starting, the line is still black.

…Not so long after your birth you were chaperoned around in your toy-sized infant car seat, and an old man ogling you on his way out of the supermarket and on the way to his demise asked, "How old is she?"

"She is only one month," replied your father, proudly beaming.

"She has a long way to go!" he exclaimed without evident envy.

Linea nigra, a black line.

4

It is almost impossible to believe that something, once non-existent and silent, is finally revealing itself. Sitting late at night in front of a blue crystal screen, I place my right hand on the crown of the world's head (on the plastic back of my warm, amenable mouse) switching languages and shuffling events, playing with a necklace of Internet links, jumping from recovered paintings looted by the Nazis to Nabokov's Berlin in the twenties, and from a Sumatra disaster to South America's currency gains. My left hand is on top of my belly, detecting movements which just weeks ago were absent. But you had already lived in my womb for several full months.

For those months nobody heard you as you held your umbilical breath.

You were like a planet that, as everybody knows, exists, but no one has ever been there.

How, out of nothing, did something come?

Or, as your Italian father's ikebana teacher would say in her brazenly broken English, "How out of nothingness came this mind-blowing somethingness?"

The world looks distant and disengaged. Its sultry surface facing me seems to be uneventful. News reports invariably have to do with somebody else. In my life, everything's neutral; even a big dog of danger is neutered; nothing is new.

But now I'm made aware that something seemingly absent for more than four months (no quickening, no quirky karate kicks) had actually hidden itself and, before the time struck, did not indicate its portentous presence. Could it be that what we consider the lack of miraculousness just hesitates to make itself evident?

In California, in the evenings after my comfy computer petrifaction at a 9-to-5 high-tech firm, I wasn't used to lifting my head up. Those few basic aluminum-colored stars hiding behind our domestic negligent smog failed to capture my interest—but in Hawaii, happily pregnant and unemployed, I ascended Mauna Kea and, deposited into the freezing darkness with a cup of free tea from the Gemini observatory, wrapped in a warm cocoon of fleece clothes under a sclerotic sky covered with a silver web of capillaries—multitudes and multitudes of unreachable planets—realized that there are many invisible things.

It is never "nothing"—because something hides itself all the time.

5

Is there any connection between a child and a fruit?

Or have I myself become a fruitful tree?

In a magazine for future mothers I read: "Your uterus is now the size of a grapefruit; your embryo is the size of a grape."

6

A graying nurse in scholarly glasses smeared purple-colored jelly on my hemispherical stomach and attached to it, with a cord's help, a metal device she held in her hand.

I was all eyes.

She moved the sophisticated rectangular box away from my blithe belly, as though protecting its unconcerned contents.

Then I was all ears.

I heard a dispersed, shapeless, shy noise and waited for more. Finally, a limping rhythm, unsure of its delicate self, got on track, and I heard precise, clear heart beats.

I had two hearts.

7

Your great grandmother was restless and crazy, but she had lived in a time of unrest.

When the war with Finland came, she was settled right on the border with Finland; when the Leningrad blockade started, she was expecting a baby right in the middle of it—in the mad medley of it—living on the Staronevsky[1].

As the Nazis tightened their grip, the Soviets tightened their belts. And then they boiled those old cowhide belts and ate them, together with starch glue on the walls beneath the wallpaper.

In Leningrad, life dried up, diminished to the size of a shrunken dry fruit discovered on a dusty and desolate shelf by a "kozha da kosti" ("skin and bones"—that's how Russians call a person starving to death). That apricot and a tuft of spring grass that he'll eat is his lucky strike of the day.

Food was scarce and the streets scary; a ghost—an anemic, pale boy wrapped in a white bed sheet so as not to be recognized—could jump on you, bring

---

1 Staronevsky Prospect, in the center of the city.

you down into a snowdrift and take away your bread coupons. Without your hundred grams—several bread crumbs—you would die.

Your great grandmother was evacuated through the Road of Life (also known as the Road of Death, since wagons with provisions and people were relentlessly bombed), but when the war ended, she—who played romances on the guitar and read playing cards like a gypsy, and a traveling gypsy she was, with her Roman nose, romantic ties with the criminal world, restlessness, deep eyes and dark past—placed her daughter in an orphanage with rough-housing kids.

In the orphanage, my mother experienced hunger.

My one-year-old father was evacuated in the beginning of the war from Byelorussia. His relatives who remained there, who had neither the guts nor grave premonitions to leave, were led to the edge of a trench. My father's great grandfather, named Naftola, a ninety-four year old Jewish gravedigger by training, was among them and, protectively flanked on both sides by daughters and grandsons, probably did not care why those graves were not properly made. In seconds, all of them were dead and covered up by the earth.

When my father grew up, all he talked about during family reunions was hunger and food.

How in exile in Novosibirsk, during those cold, bare years of war, they had a hen named Katya and a pig named Borya, and how poor Katya and Borya had to be eaten.

When I visit my parents' apartment, which looks like a resourcefully stocked grocery store, I stumble upon cans and canisters on the floor.

I flounder counting dollar-store food containers.

Carrots and nuts, goat's milk, garlic, meticulously washed blueberries in plastic jars, that I have to bring back after consuming this deliriously desperate feast— for them to replenish.

And they are replenished themselves by knowing that they can play a part.

8

My Italian mother-in-law, in every way distant, sits somewhere in her sterile flat in Turin, ecstatic that her grandson caught chicken pox. "I'm so excited he's sick, she explains into a phone receiver. He has to stay home, and I will babysit. Finally, I will be useful."

My father stands in front of me in his subsidized studio in San Francisco and tests a baby sling. It smells like cheap soap, like a thrift store. He stands in front of me and demonstrates, while my mother scolds him for putting the sling on the wrong way.

Then he hands me a dreadful, old-fashioned potty made from bruised, weathered wood. Surely, it served generations of kids. My arthritic mother artistically sits and pretends to defecate.

"It cost five bucks at a garage sale, but a seller 'long-changed' us so that we "earned" five dollars instead[2]," my mother says and continues: "For that money we could purchase one more for our future granddaughter to use here during her visits. But your sister spoiled everything."

And she tells me about my sis, who, being so serious after a miscarriage about everything having to do with children, cried out upon realizing the mishap: "It is for a baby! It is a bad omen!" and ran back to return the folded bills.

During the times of physical changes (in my pregnant body, in my sister's malfunctioning body, in the aging bodies of my agile mother and father), vulnerability looms like never before. I can't fit myself behind the steering wheel, I weep tying my shoes, I slip in the bathtub, I slowly lower myself to the edge of the bed, I bend, trying not to hurt my enormous belly. I'm overwhelmed by an inability to do simple things when the complex job of creating a person takes place inside.

Enveloping the baby, I feel and look very fragile, and my parents become more paternal but also pathetic.

As though the new life turning within me gives their life a different turn.

9

After a visit with my observant obstetrician, I stare

---

2 They gave him ten dollars; he thought it was twenty, and gave them fifteen in change.

at tantalizingly temperamental teenagers outside a bike shop and ponder if I can relate to any of them.

Margalit, will you look like these giddy girls when grown up? Or like those broody or brawling boys? In the future there might be a similarity between you and them, but what bothers me in the present is that you already seem distant.

But how can I feel related to you? There is nothing yet to place on or under a pillow (perhaps, your hospital wrist band or the first diaper shirt) or hug for the night. Surprisingly, I do not even have to follow rules on how to expand a placenta; how to divide growing cells; how to direct them toward your eyes, kidneys, or foot. Everything had already been set by somebody else— and I felt left out of business.

Therefore, to discover how to relate to you in the future, to that you who is now inside (in the womb), I turn outside (to the world).

I'm peeping at proverbial pimples, boys' low pants and girls' posh pumps, and I feel no connection to them.

On realizing it, I get very frustrated, imagining that there will be, at your birth, no connection to you.

10

A girl from New York, a thriving transplant who had learned an extinct language in Russia (in college, she studied Yiddish, and I—the more viable, virulent Hebrew), casually cautioned me that once my daughter was born, my life would be never the same.

Meaning that piles of poop-stained diapers would shield me from creating fastidious fiction, and baby babbles or cries—from the New Yorker's cartoons I flip through before falling asleep: this activity lets me skim characters and situations while staying firmly anchored to a bed

That your breast-sucking will be like a sanction, a sanction to stop being myself, because my life will never be the same either… because now everything would change!

I will be attached by my nipple to you and won't be able to move, when you, in your turn, will be like a puppy who does not want to let go of a glove or a lopsided ball, taking a firm stand on all fours, snarling while the owner tries to retrieve the slobbered-on thing (the slobbered-on thing in this case is my chewed-up breast)

Keeping an eye on you, I will not be able to keep an eye on myself or the world

A sudden tunnel tired vision that I will develop—

A soccer mom's visor will be firmly positioned over my unmade-up eyes

It will be like SIDS, the sudden infant death syndrome that will overcome me, meaning that after delivering an infant, I myself will die and never have my own life, apart from a newly minted newborn

No bold, borderline books that I want to relive

No faraway countries rising like ghosts from those

bold books, whose grass is being trampled, like book pages, under my feet, when I finally reach a different continent

No open-air blues concerts with summer drunks lining up in front of port-o-potty green cabins, draining the last water drips from plastic faucets while listening to sad, rhythmic songs chock-full of choked back tears and color

No instant success from my literary stunts, from my bipolar, borderline books, which would bring me the means to go to different continents—which, in turn, would bring me more ideas for books

No blues but baby blues—that's what the NY girl says

That's what she warned me about while permanently glued to her white carton house in a cartoonishly tame neighborhood of exclusively white, bleachy pale whitish neighbors having no sun and no blues

Did HER life ever change?

11

It's as if a fishing bob suddenly dives, and something inside me—the bait, perhaps—is instantly swallowed by a persistent, strong fish...

It's as if a frog tries to surface, pounding water with its limp, little legs while gurgling and reaching the top of the pond to gasp some fresh air...

It's as if one takes a polished chestnut speckled with

sunlight, one of those that are infinitely being carried in a pocket in hopes for finite luck, and shakes it, hearing how something inside it knocks and rolls shyly and gently...

Everything goes into a boisterous, boiling pan of word witchery: simmering waters trembling under the sun; crawling crickets touching things with their cautious moustache; a round, firm bee's nest pulsing under an open palm...

One can evoke the whole animal world with its cryptic nature and creatures to describe what is going on.

But it is only a new baby busily moving inside me.

12

At night, I cannot sleep.

In those popular preparatory books they say that when a mother is awake, her fetus is usually dozing; when a mother is sound asleep, the unsupervised fetus starts to hiccup and kick.

Not true with us. We are in sync.

You are restlessly swimming and almost knocking me over, water splashing in the womb.

I am reckless, letting myself rock on the nightly insomnia waves.

Prior to your conception, I segregated my dark self from the world; days passed in prostration, procrastination, contemplation or writing. Single-handedly, I faced the dreaded duality of the day, when routine would overcome depth.

Have you ever watched how a mother and daughter, arms around each other's shoulders or waists, go to another room to confide secret tales? They need that seclusion; they unite to discuss.

Only several months pregnant, I am alone, but inside me there is one more me, and it adds a different quality to my solitude.

13

…Waking up worried: where are those wiggly movements and wobbly karate kicks?

…Living as a schizophrenic, as it is perfectly normal to sense in your wholesome body somebody else, to paranoiacally listen to "voices," to panic when not hearing gurgling or tapping…

It's all in reverse: a mental patient is considered healed when they finally convince him that he is alone, when he is not guided by illegitimate ghosts; when he becomes so incensed and thick-skinned that he ceases paying attention to voices or stops believing in little people inside his stomach or head…

On the contrary, many lend a sympathetic ear to a woman who claimed that she had heard her child's "voice"; who, still pregnant, imagined him grown up, coloring her mildly grey, monotonous middle-age.

A man hearing voices suspects that he is becoming

insane. Sensing a separate life inside her, a woman is jubilant.

And in this case, it's not a phantom—it's a fetus.

14

A fur- and sugar-coated man from putinesque Russia, an avid reader and an avian traveler, surely knows the mystery of a woman from very afar… he is not the first male to inform me that an expectant woman is extremely autistic: she is oblivious of everything while transfixed on her own transfiguring shape.

Men offer thoughts about the miracle of motherhood. About lips whispering to the whale of a belly. About an inspired gait and a peculiar gaiety, about the brightening of a future mom's face—"as though a Madonna's."

I belch, bellow at my Italian husband and move slowly, heavily, as though carrying a yoke, no lightness in view.

For me the lightening is when a baby is supposed to "drop": this happens when his head starts its customary descent into the pelvis.

Today my stern, steel-nerved obstetrician (the best surgeon in the department, they tell me) jokes that I'm carrying a basketball player—she is so elongated, he says, that he could even touch the tip of her head with his fingers (fingering me).

That probably means, he speculates, that she dropped and is ready for a new world, a new womb.

How big is the opening?—I ask him.

He answers: two fingers.

According to old wives' tales and moth-balled myths, a pregnancy is something hidden, unknown—but this is a passer-by's view. From my point of view, it's mundane manufacturing (counting movements, measuring the uterus, taking a certain number of vitamins and, after thirty five, a certain number of risks); it is motherhood math.

15

Kneeling, your future father looks, from underneath, at my bare belly and says that this marble globe, this moving miniature mountain reminds him of our instincts and of the Stone Age.

He says that when we need to perform primitive calculations, we purchase a powerful Pentium.

When we feel a deep need to connect to somebody, we don't hold hands—we hook up shallow cables.

When we desire healing, we don't pray, because we preach pills.

But this bloated belly reminds us that we are from flesh.

That we have something primordial—it's not orderly circuits or irksome iPods flicked off by remote control; it is something that develops with diligence, despite our bad grades in Chemistry, Genetics, or Genesis.

"Listen, he says to me, isn't it wondrous? Those cells

divide regardless of our trust in divinity, and the body of a fetus matures whether or not we are mature enough to raise a new human being."

And when he climbs the steps of these high-flown words, I nervously click my way through Web sites and sink down a dark well of diagnoses:

1)   prolapsed cord
2)   low amniotic fluid
3)   fetal distress
4)   torn sac, slow heartbeat
5)   mermaid legs
6)   spina bifida
7)   two-headed monsters

We are both talking about the same thing: the intricate forces of nature.

16

It emerged so effortlessly; it was never important.

On its own something was going on, unannounced in the first few days or maybe few weeks.

Still, despite this ease, my body revolted: two nights in a row I was rolling on a cool Peruvian rug as on burning coals, with a pain burrowing into my lower back—an embryo, as a mole, was burrowing down the uterus lining.

There was almost no will there—it was a passive

submission to chance, a zygote roulette.

But when a clump of cells grew bigger, pity grew together with it.

Bellowing to protect a protruding belly from my spouse's elbows; pushing him away when he trespassed on my side of the bed. There was a pity toward what was within, the pity toward a pit placed there by an invisible, yet inquisitive, force.

Pity and hate.

When I hated myself, I hated it together with me because it shared my dull days and daily depression— but I loathed it only when I considered it to be a part of me. When I thought it to be separate—a unique human being with its own bent—I had high expectations.

And shivered reading a horror story about a loony who wanted a baby of her own so much that she slaughtered a woman and cut out of her a full-grown fetus... Like it was an organ not needed, like an appendix.

I was going slowly on freeways; I pushed the steering wheel with an airbag far away from myself; I sit on a pillow—to keep the baby invincible in case of a car crash.

Something that appeared there by chance (that zany zygote roulette, a twenty-five percent probability every month that a healthy woman from eighteen to thirty five years of age faces by flipping a coitus coin) now was becoming my choice.

Now I wanted it badly.

17

An expectant mother limits the activities she undertakes during the day: no casual sex, no casual wining and raw food dining, nor sightseeing from an unpressurized cabin of a helicopter or scuba diving, no lifting of weights.

No lifting of a world's wanton burden on swayed back shoulders; no accessory sadness tipping off her center of gravity (she already has trouble performing her belly-balancing act).

Taking a fetus' future in her own hands, she consumes great amounts of organic health foods, strongly believing that this will give him a high IQ and an ability to endure high altitude soccer. To make him succeed, for the three-fourths of the year everything should be tranquil.

Thus, sacrificial sacramental parents assume they must limit their horizons to widen those of the newborn.

18

A would-be baby reminds me of danger.

From high school I brought home doggy bags of biology knowledge: meiosis, mitosis, splitting hairs over a double helix, division of cells. Dangers awaiting my daughter inside me (now she is busily duplicating her DNA strands) differ from those that catch me on the outside.

I see myself with a stroller walking blightly lit streets. What if a shabby white man dressed in bleak black (or a brightly-dressed black man with the whites of his eyes blazing) approaches me with a knife. I would be scared to death.

This summer in China, somewhere near the remote remnants of the Great Chinese Wall, we let our dutiful chauffeur take a well-deserved rest (confused by our desire to be left alone, he continued to slowly dribble after us in his dusty "Datsun") and walked empty-handed on an empty road. Only a beat-up car loaded with scary large stones (one fell, jumped high as a ball several times and landed at our feet) or a horse carriage with people of unknown intentions and destinations would pass by, and, giving them way, we stepped onto the dirt.

The buildings around us seemed to be aged military barracks, which, after their retirement, applied for another position—just to be useful. As we could see from afar, children's clothes hung on invisible strings, men swaggered in sweatpants; at that moment, far away from my land of origin, I felt omnipotent, happy.

A strange, non-linear force of fate brought me first to Kazakhstan and then to China—it was impersonated by a wheel-chaired or, better, wheel-chained woman who could not walk herself, but who gave me a gift of being airborne. Olga, whose petite, pitifully fragile, fleshless body was overcompensated by overly large glasses and an acute intellect, arranged a generous grant for me, and I landed first in Almaty, and then Beijing.

My plane could fall in Almaty, in Astana, in Beijing, in Xian.

Back in the U.S., peering into a Kazakhstan life reflected in ripples of Internet news, I read that a flight engineer in Almaty came too close to a plane engine and was sucked in by a freak force. In the city of Beijing there was bird flu and in some villages—leeches poisoning the waters (in China, we were afraid not of criminals, but of creatures: if any native touched a tourist, he could end up in the hands of a firing squad).

Walking through the Forbidden City with a large yellow umbrella with a tattoo on its leg ("this protection from the Sun is donated to plain folk by the president"), I ran risks (which were implied rather than implemented): to be burned by sun rays, to be bitten by an insect, to be hit by a stone before it found solace at our feet destroying the car bumper of our guide.

And what about you, Margalit? The same way I miscarried many promising projects, I could have miscarried you, too. If a spermatozoon rushed to the left instead of the right, when an egg was waiting for it on another sidewalk, like on a blind date which went geographically wrong even before being consummated—you would not be born. What if chromosomes, cosmoses in themselves, did not pair as needed… what if I paired with a different man?

If my cervix were somewhat "incompetent"; if I had a mioma or tumor; if my placenta would be too thin or too old… How many times in a bathroom stall I was afraid that with too much straining you would end up squeezed out; how in the shower I stared into murky, mad waters trying to see if you had fallen…

At any moment an embryo can meet a sudden, sad death; it is preyed upon by the same misfortunes that plague adults: bad nutrition, wrong timing, unforeseen circumstances, not enough faith.

19

Margalit overcomes all the rules of geometry: from a round shape ("you look like you engulfed a cannonball," a passerby informs me), from a hardened coconut of my belly she constructs a square, showing at once all her extremities.

What is this one: a hand, a foot, a hard head or a soft butt?

My belly extends every possible way—at a visit to the obstetrician, when I strive to align my hard-to-operate body (it's like a complex mechanism with its buttons not working) in the middle of a tissue-covered chair, she jerks to the right, crumpled under the right dome of the uterus, visible as a fish under a thick layer of water.

I feel as though she unabashedly puts herself on display. As though, under inquisitive obstetrical eyes, it's not a fetus, but my internal organ—a kidney or a colon—extending to show its brazenly angular and firm forms through my stretched skin...

I am ashamed.

When she was only four gestational months, she ran away from a rude, rowdy African-American doctor who scared her while attaching a device to listen to her heartbeat. He tried placing it on different spots (I gasped upon hearing silence—is she still there?)—and each time she ran away. She moved inside me eluding his roughness, and I, finally relieved and relaxed after sensing her activities and her acting up, watched with pleasure his impatient and startled face.

When I turn to my left, the left side of my uterus gets heavier as though a cannon ball were slowly rolling into a niche; the left side of the belly grows a bump.

She is not comfortable.

When I turn to my right, I feel funny on the left side: at the moment when she finally finds a new position, when she does not expect any more changes, her cozy capsule betrays her and shifts again.

She is again bothered with no evident reason. And again she has to move.

She can achieve convenient coziness if she follows me: if I turn onto my left, she needs to take a seat on the left; if I turn to my right, she has to shift right; otherwise, she just hangs for her dear life onto uterus walls, like a cat balancing on all fours on an inclined table.

Thus, before her "outer" life even starts, she already has to adjust to her mom… Should I simply outweigh her?

Rather, we have to listen to each other's desires. When I turn without giving her a timely warning, I feel painful discomfort: she tries to keep herself in her former position, her hands and feet, as cat's claws, scratch my innards.

I must proceed slowly, with caution and intuition, repositioning myself inch by inch, inkling by inkling, as though instructing her on what's going to happen next…

This tactic should continue when she is born.

20

A fresh sensation of newness—such clean air—when leaving home, as though a traveler, with a bulky, big-bellied "hospital" bag.

Gates automatically open. No metal noise. It is still quiet. It's seven a.m.

The world has been already informed.

I always had this very same feeling when leaving the obnoxious, boxy apartment complex for Patagonia or Tahiti: something is ready to happen, but you don't know what to expect.

Planes from the nearby airport fly over the Bay, flounder in the mirroring water and add to my feeling of transit. Or transition, perhaps. Black gates and blue bay right in front are the same, yet they are transformed. As in my childhood, at the end of summer when we fled to a city flat from a cold dacha... even the linoleum seemed strange, compared in my mind to the chinky floors at the countryside.

The orderly flat, left on its own for three summer months, had had to learn how to embrace people again. Now, after a long separation, it looked unrecognizable (water pipes crossly grumble when turned on for the first time after a break), and the unused, vacant air was not yet mixed with our breath... Nothing is changed, but our minds have the ability to experience things as though new.

Then, in this transformed or, better, transfixed, world, she appears, snub-nosed and silky. Tightly holding new limbs, snuggling up to platelets and lymph, I'm suddenly enveloped by sympathy toward withered women who once were newborns.

After Margalit's birth I read in a newspaper, almost turned into a police blog to attract receding spores of readers, about a high society lady who had lost her husband in the war in Korea. She was sweet and demented. Young girls in their twenties, gangly gang members in blue baseball uniforms (their rivals favored maroon jerseys), befriended her and moved to her flat. From there they sold crack and routinely turned away social workers who came to check on the old lady and do her household chores.

The sweet lady emanated a bad smell; her potty

had never been emptied; her sheets were not changed; her mattress sported bedsores. She attempted to call the police but hadn't enough memory to continue a comprehensible conversation. She would phone, say "hi" and then hesitate, clinging to her own words and forgetting what she wanted to say.

Months passed before the gang fooling this frail, ailing woman was caught. During the court hearings, it was revealed that girly gang members ate the meager meals brought to the poor widow and even scolded the social workers that it was not tasty. The widow had lost so much weight that she could hardly walk.

Peering into her parchment-like face in the newspaper, I felt pity for her, since now I knew that once she was as innocent, helpless and silky as a baby fresh from the womb, exactly like Margalit.

21

Making good use of vegetation, the book states: "It takes a lot of pushing and stretching to move a baby the size of a melon through a cervical opening that starts out the size of a kidney bean."

22

Lying feverishly in a hospital bed a few hours after delivery, I visualize, again and again, the bewildered look on her frantic face... on her face with unfocused blue eyes and a mouth in the shape of a triangle (even mute, it moves, sending me signals)…

Seeing in my mind's eye her first appearance in this world, I meekly smile, knowing that right at this moment she sleeps in her see-through glass menagerie nearby.

This is the person, who is already drastically different (and several hours older) from the one who emerged from my womb.

This one, looking in her protective container like a shiny museum exhibit on a display, has a fuller face and less puffy eyes than the one placed on my breast by nurses excited by her perfection ("Oh that hair, oh those eyelashes, her beauty is so unreal that she looks like a doll!"). This one already learned how to root straight for my breast, whereas the first one was disoriented in her new world and cried when they tried to orchestrate the moment of closeness.

This growth of life is perceived by my quirky mind as two parallel life events: one minutes, or moments, before (already stored in memory) and another that takes place just this second (in front of my eyes).

The one before (how she emerged after almost tearing my legs apart, how I exclaimed, disoriented, to laughing nurses, "She has such a big tongue!", how I looked at her, but she was looking away, occupied because her skin color was inspected and her hair was washed) is a rich source of memories.

The one that is now (how she snores in her

cuvette, how I adjust to my flat stomach) is full of unpredictability, it is full of the future.

23

She was born a strong girl: she could almost hold her head upright from the first moments of life; she kicked an old, ladylike nurse who tried to wrap her in a used hospital blanket.

She played with her tongue; she already had all the reflexes: grasping the needle a RN poked her with, flinching when touched, annoyed when hungry, crying when wet. She immediately started crawling on my breast on all fours like a kitten, meanwhile entangling herself in my gold chain.

She jumped into life not wasting time, ready to act.

But a gap in perception, a delay between two points in space, the hole between two generations showed herself in her Grandma.

For Margalit, it did not take long to get adjusted to a different life, coming from a dark, confined hollow into a lighted world hallway: she immediately started sucking colostrum and wetting a colossal number of diapers. But it took a much longer time for her Grandma before her motherly milk flowed.

In the beginning, grandmother fussed, refusing to show compassion and motherly camaraderie toward her daughter who was a couple of months short of becoming a mother herself. She said that if there was no morning sickness, the pregnancy was a piece of cake. She said that nobody visited her in a maternity ward—why should she then? Then she proclaimed that perhaps it wasn't worthwhile for her to travel so far to see something that she remembers so closely: her own motherhood.

But as soon as she received the midnight call, she jumped on the last train and appeared in the hospital ward, despite all her earlier warnings that grandmothers and long commutes don't go together.

In no time she was sitting on her daughter's bed, peering intently into her granddaughter's cuvette with words that *her* afterbirth stitches healed right away with no residue and that *her* children did not cry at night. Her children's diapers were cleaner, their hair much longer, their skin smoother; their stumps fell in three days.

She remembered very well that her milk flowed like a river, her blood after delivery went away like a tide, her baby stopped making sad faces as soon as she would wave her right hand.

Overall, it was a sharp contrast: her granddaughter's instincts kicked in right away, but her own motherly— or grandmotherly—instincts took time to surface, saddened, hardened, restrained by her hard and long life.

24

They all ask: after it passed, what can you say about your motherly feelings, your instincts? How were those nine months?

They all know the known, but whatever is known by them is simply not true. "Nine months is nothing except a physiological marathon," I address those who bought a familiar story of mother's glow and gnawing love. "The body does everything by itself; you have no control. It struggles, it stretches, it stringently aches. The days are measured by weight gain, heavy breasts, high blood pressure, the heavy burden of a womb, by a baby's heartbeat."

It is society—I say—that paints a rosy motherhood with blushing cheeks. It is simply not like that. A mother cannot love what she has yet to inspect. You have to know somebody to love them.

For me, there were no dreams—who will this baby be? There were no dreams of family vacations, of Chanukah gifts, of a son "who will be a mother's protector." Or of a grown girl playing the violin. My body was simply full with a baby; my mind was mulling over this white monitor, those black lines…

Then I stop short: if it is only a physiological marathon, why, instead of catching my breath when crossing a bumpy, rambunctious field, am I trying to catch every thought that crosses my mind?

25

On New Year's Eve you turned nine months, and your great grandfather turned ninety six—or, if we would clock him, we'd say "four until a hundred."

In your age, you count birthdays by months: on the first of each month, your grandparents visit and bring you a cake with several candles, something that you, still satisfied by mother's milk and baby purees, had no use for.

In your great grandfather's condition, his children celebrated every day of his life: his cancer, for a while in a remission, returned in full force.

On New Year's Eve, gathered around a big table with kosher wine and smoked fish somewhat gentrified by mixed marriages and Russian pierozhki, your great grandfather's family marked the new year: if nothing happened during it, that would be good news.

This extended family was together in Russia, always gathering and gossiping about each other's salaries or salad recipes, and they brought this tradition to the U.S.. In the new country, they were still holding grudges against each other, but going strong.

They gathered around your great grandfather, their placid, pale, weak patriarch. Always in an elegant suit, with a wide-brimmed hat and a tie, this time he was dressed in a brand-new coordinated sweatpants and sweatshirt. This was the sign that this year for him would surely be different. His doctor informed the immediate family that in his condition people may live only days or months.

We did not know what gift to bring him for his birthday: his needs at the last stage of his life were simple and bare. Why clutter his apartment with rubbish? So we gave him a beautifully framed picture of his great granddaughter, who, in a sense, was his last big achievement.

He took it in his tired hands covered by pigmentation and said: "Good, very good." Till very recently he, who came to the U.S. in his late seventies, tried to take classes in English. And he said the word "good" in English—always staying in perfect mental, though no longer, physical, shape.

Then he started eating his birthday cake, carefully dissecting it with a teaspoon, but could not finish. He was too weak and had to go rest in a bedroom. He left the holiday table right at the moment we produced our cameras to take his picture holding his great granddaughter.

Then we decided to wait till he woke up—to take this last picture of the youngest and the oldest of the family clan.

But when he woke up, his nine-month-old great granddaughter, overwhelmed by a big number of relatives previously not seen by her, crumpled in my arms, with hair wet from heat and exhaustion, sound asleep.

Now you both were falling asleep frequently, in the

most unusual places and times.

You—in your playpen, on top of a plush toy; your great grandfather—in an armchair, holding your picture and asking the pronunciation of your Italian middle name.

When you were old enough to pronounce his name, he was dead.

26

The night we brought you home from an impersonal hospital room, where we counted the hours and how many times you wet diapers, I was awakened, not by your cries (you slept soundly in your bassinet), but by your father's exalted and wheezing whispers.

He was saying, "She walks, she walks, she walks!"

I placed a hand on his wet, as though sprayed from a pulverizer, hot forehead, and he woke up. He told me that he saw you in a dream, the real you with your lithe, little, languid, lanugoed body—and that you walked, just several days old! He was foreseeing skills you would acquire as you grew, and he was already scared to death of these rapid changes, even in dreams.

The next morning, he touched a dark pigmented path running from my belly button… Once the dear dweller left its coconut-shaped uterus shell, the womb shrank, and the *linea nigra*, not stretched anymore, widened and paled.

He said, "I can't wait to see what ending you added

to your fictitious story… after all these perturbations of labor… after she is finally born!"

What "ending" did he expect? It is true that the sueded pigmented line soon will be no more; it will disappear without a trace; scars will heal; previously tight tissues will soften, and with the introduction of solid food (crackers or carrots) the infant will stop looking like an undernourished invertebrate (perhaps a frog)—and will look plentiful, promising, plump.

According to my pregnancy book, after running its course, the *linea nigra* will turn into *linea alba*, a white line. It will be indistinguishable from the white plains of a warm and wide belly.

And this whiteness—a witness to fear of the unknown—teaches me: anything can happen; nothing or nobody is set in stone; nothing is written yet, because for both mother and a daughter the page starts anew:

Like a mother, a daughter also has a white line.

SWITCH

1

ELSA TRIOLET

As eloquently as she used to string words together,
now she threaded beads.

Words were abundant, but money scarce: she was
a Russian émigré stripped of Motherland and mother
of pearls, future and furs, and her husband a French
writer resourceful with syntax yet not with corporate
syndicates.

Starving for the time to write, she plotted designs of
decorative necklaces, and breadcrumbs on the family
table were soon swept away and replaced by solid loaves
of wealth. He was swept off his feet by her beauty.

She fortified him with *croque-monsieurs* and *foie-
gras*, and herself—with the power gained by her ability
to combine things, to knit a circle of co-dependency,
to create a safety net with her words. Still, in recurring
nightmares she would fall into the bottomless pit of her
Russian.

As a youth, she frequented cabarets and cafés, favored
ballet posters and products for hair, and her flirting
with local photographers was interspersed with flashes
of passion (one of them left us this snapshot where she
impersonates a Greek goddess). Exalted exhaustion was
shared by all of her friends who used to arrive home at

5 a.m. after discussing Catullus, the carriage dragged by a disheveled horse and disapproving *muzhik*.

When she fled the Bolsheviks, she changed her name from Ella to Elsa, where the sneaked-in "s" stood for "escape" (or for "escargot"). Her body was a fine-tuned instrument receptive to feelings. Before marrying the writer, she'd hooked up with an affable officer named André Triolet and went with him to Tahiti, where she'd recline on the couch and read.

Every resuscitated Russian word—*sobaka*, *ruzh'e*, or *kolodetz*—made her heart race, which led to nausea. In St. Petersburg, a piece of coarse paper swept up by the wind ended up at her feet; she picked it up. The paper read, "Ammunition Report. Used three bullets, wounded one and killed two. Did not waste anything." A soldier passing by stared at her with severity, and she held her skirt with both hands making sure it was not riding up.

Russian for her became: hot flashes, shivers, bittersweet memories of the soapy nursery, and only rarely—a full, round happiness, a fruit torn from a tree by a child's impatient hand (other apples fell to the ground with a dull thump; the family estate was soon filled with intruders). In Tahiti, her Russian mixed with the hot air of unloved tropical monotony: in the mornings, André would dress up and leave to check the other islands; she would be alone, with words. When they made love, what he muttered in the heat of passion was in an unintelligible language—still, she could read him as easily as a page, which openly stated, "You are not one of my main interests."

She addressed her letters about Tahiti to somebody else.

2

Zinaida Shakhovskoy

At four, with a large pink bow in her blonde platinum hair, she introduced herself to an inarticulate toddler of two, who clumsily walked along the dusty path in her family's park, "My name is Zinaida, and I speak Russian, German, and French," and she waited politely for his response, but he continued walking in total oblivion, ending up on all fours. She stood there with her three languages, open-mouthed.

That summer, she taught a handful of simple French words to a flock of shoeless boys, who used to fish from a half-sunken bridge, and promised to show them *Tour Eiffel*. They didn't believe her, and when she approached them the next morning, they threw rotten fish heads at her and shouted something obscene.

When she was six, her stutter became prominent, but only in Russian: at first, her *nyanya*, thick-cheeked and slow-thinking Tatiana, decided that it was due to Zinaida's fear of Baba-Yaga, the histrionic and evil hero of fairytales with a hooked nose and crooked intentions. Later, it became evident that the debilitating stutter wouldn't go away, and Zinaida began to spend lonely days in the library. Somehow her language skills were better on paper, and books didn't mind if they were slowly read.

Her parents would protect her from the outer world by switching to Pig Latin when their daughter burst into the room and happened upon a conversation, saying: "Stepan went *unting-hay* and he *illed-kay* a big *kuropatka*," and Zinaida would stare at them, not understanding what bearded *dyadya* Stepan did to the bird. She didn't dare to ask.

The stutter—which made the accumulation of thoughts in her head almost painful—also made her invisible when two sailors led away her mother, a tidy miniature woman in a strapped dress, with Zinaida staying in the corner unnoticed. She was eleven.

In the evening of the same day her two beloved dogs, white-tailed Bubie and one-eared Feofan (she treated him with sugar and herbs when a monstrous mongrel tore off his left ear), got poisoned because of their high-pitched barking, "an obstacle to the Revolution"—or at least this is what Zinaida overheard through an open window. This time, nobody switched syllables in the word "killed"; it was uttered in thick, stocky Russian, "*Ubili.*"

It was the shrill autumn of 1917 when yellow, red, and green leaves covered the paths in the park, and there was nobody to remove them, as their gardener lay in bed with a fever, after being shot by strangers that night when he went out to check on a suspicious noise. Tatiana, who told the fairytales about Baba Yaga, left the premises and never came back. A young, scrawny sailor with dirt under his nails, yet wearing a white linen shirt a couple of sizes too big, brought the news, "Do you know how to keep a secret? Your mother's alive."

Zinaida scribbled a note and gave it to him with a coin, "Mama, I hope you'll come back very soon, I'm here waiting for you, I don't know where to go." The sailor took the note and disappeared without even a nod, but the next day she saw him again.

Lonely and eager to talk, he started visiting her every night.

3

MARGARITA MEKLINA

She felt his failure as if it were hers: a dried up, single vegetable on a grocery shelf, its end dangling and wrinkled, in a plastic bag full of air making up for the absence of flesh. Her breasts, when she sat on him bending forward, would elongate like two drops of water ready to fall from the metal edge of a roof, and swing—empty and useless. She'd sit there, holding an unstable thing in her hand, and see herself from afar, as in a vision: trying to use a stick shift in a car without innards that wouldn't oblige.

Besides a non-virile husband, she had a virtual lover. His name was Ethan Tanner; he was sixteen years her senior and worked for a Jewish organization unearthing the past. Later at work, with an unfilled physical void, she mentioned the words "White Power" in her e-letter to him, both intrigued and unnerved by his sudden interest in her, a Russian author muted by life in the U.S.: "Why did you give me, a stranger from Twitter, your home address? What if behind a JPEG façade of a freckled girl, a poster child for fantasies, there hides a rough-skinned extremist, magnetized by your Nazi hunting activities?"

Dismissing her fears with laughter, he retrieved her from the silence of the Web via Skype and invited her to his summer home in Boston, "remodeled and ready for pleasures"; she politely declined; yet, this invitation, and envisioning him in sexual scenarios, cross-pollinated her memories of that morning, when she had tried to extract strength from what was buried under four years of a mellow marriage.

That evening, she heard on the news that a White Power supremacist shot a black guard at the Boston Jewish Museum. She felt nauseous from this crazed juxtaposition of evil power (blood and blind hate) with kind weakness, when she was covered, instead of kisses, with her husband's ardent apologies. Her ego deflated, she thought of the black guard as a readily available target (he had kindly opened the door for an approaching elderly gentleman in a bulky trench coat) but an elusive metaphor.

The ailing killer considered gas chambers a myth, yet he shot into another myth, the idea of equality for all races, as though it were a tangible target. Newspapers described the white man as a "frustrated artist with a fake college diploma who'd lost his retirement savings" (he was taken away on a gurney); the black man was "a young man who'd just started a family" (they left him on the ground, and the pool of his blood gleamed ominously next to his shiny shoes and massive gold watch).

The vision of clear plastic wrapped around weak flesh disturbed her together with the vision of a man shooting into an idea as two examples of the futility of human existence. She poured her Californian plum wine with the Japanese name into a clear glass, sat cross-legged in her captain's chair from a local IKEA and tried to turn disgust into digest, describing her inklings, but her Russian was too raw, too close to the skin, and she started feeling much worse.

She checked her e-mail, images of a failed effort in bed, and of the elderly white supremacist playing in her mind simultaneously as in a video clip. Words mentioned by chance in her earlier e-mail found their mirror match in Ethan's new message: "The security precautions at 'Jewish Justice' have been stepped up, because we were informed that a handful of our employees have been added to the White Power's list."

4

Zinaida Shakhovskoy

The scrawny sailor noticed that the girl was a stutterer but it didn't stop him from retelling her every minute of his daily existence. Entering her room, he'd grab a piece of cake or a pear that she'd saved after a routine raid of the servants' kitchen and claim that it was more important for him to be satiated than for her, "who just sits here doing nothing all day."

He repeatedly said, "I'm so puny that the water pushes me out; I'll dive deeper if I eat more." Even before he told her his story of a cold-blooded eyewitness, she had heard about White Army officers caught on board of the ship: they were seized, interrogated (there was nothing they could say that was unknown; all they could repeat was *"Slava Otechestvu"* and spit into the Bolsheviks' eyes), and then thrown into the sea with weights tied to their feet.

She listened wide-eyed to the sailor, who counted the circles on the water when the first officer went into the sea. Then he counted more, standing on board the ship in awe of this exercise in the extermination of enemies. "Some of them went with their feet first and some head-first, but we didn't care," he exclaimed, strangely excited. "Like they never cared about us, the poor and under-privileged," he emphasized, and looked at her as though adding extra earnestness to his words.

Every night, coming to her with a new message from the jail where her mother was kept, he made her pay for these messages with science lessons; his almost visceral interest in "how things are" (she wouldn't have been surprised if he had suggested cutting her into pieces just to see how everything inside her worked) made her nauseous, but she could not escape. He claimed that since she was well-educated "in the school for the rich," now the time had come to relay her knowledge and skills to him, the son of a factory worker, who would take this knowledge and build the new world.

With her stutter, she struggled telling him things and would simply draw the planets or show him how to read the barometer in a dining room and predict weather, and this was enough to satisfy his needs in science. Curious, he wanted to know what happens to human bodies when they stop breathing and talking, and he continued diving into the deep waters in the place where the officers were thrown into the sea.

For three weeks, he continued bringing her notes from her mother's jail cell (her last words were, "I'm going to be executed tomorrow") and would say, "Your mother is still alive and the officers are still dead. They hadn't changed much since yesterday." The next day, when she didn't know what to think after her mother's grim message, the scrawny sailor met her with the words, "Your mother's released and the officers' bodies are now becoming disfigured, even though I can still clearly see their feet and the stones attached." In her mind, she saw murky waters and bodies, mutilated and shapeless, yet still in uniform, and this image of static officers lazily moving their limbs, under water pierced by sourceless sunlight, with their features smeared by deterioration, stayed with her all her life and entered one of her books.

She didn't know how to behave: to show to him that she believed him; to show her gratitude? The next day he came with her mother and said, "Your mother is finally here, and one of "my" officers, the one who was the most defiant and stocky, went away after a storm. When I lowered myself down, I didn't see him." When her mother asked for the explanation, the sailor burst into tears and ran away.

5

Elsa Triolet

Three flags waved in front of her: a Polynesian palm leaf and two tricolors, Russian and French.

On the flag of her fate, there were already three names drawn.

André would enter her room at dawn, drunk and smelling of mollusks, and he'd hit and miss frequently: first, raising her legs into the air, aiming at the wrong place and feeling resistance (she swallowed her urge to strangle him with her thighs); second, when she attempted to throw him out, he'd slap her and, having been pushed away, would rage toward her but miss in the dark.

Victor Shklovsky encountered her in Berlin but relegated his desire for her to his analytical fiction, later claiming that the love flowered only for the sake of the novel. He was a formalist who later was welcomed back by the Bolsheviks and specialized in Leo Tolstoy, his wide chest covered with government medals like gold spittles. He quoted her letters to him from Tahiti in a novel, "Zoo," and one notable mustachioed proletarian figure read it and stated, "If she weren't so bourgeois, she'd make a great writer."

Not only did she become a writer, she married one, image of two mirrors frottering and rubbing each other, reflecting surfaces lubricated by passion, like paraffin. His name was Louis Aragon. In the morning, he would take a briefcase full of necklaces (some artfully made with aspirin pills) and go to a market to sell them, quietly closing the door so as not to wake up Elsa. When she and her sister wore this homemade jewelry over their form-fitting dresses with deep décolletage, it drove men crazy. No matter their country of birth, men became speechless, Russian, German, or French giving way to a coiled and pulsing desire within.

Sister Lilya would be birdily entangled in many affairs, among them one with Mayakovsky, the poet who praised Revolutionary destruction and Stalin and got fed up with his own words, finally coughing out a bullet (he was 37, the official version of suicide being not for political reasons but for love). Elsa had to be careful in her choices of words and men—not to get distracted by extraneous, non-essential needs. Needy herself, she begged Aragon, "Are my *Necklaces* nice?"

"They are as sparkling as you are, my dear Elsa," his answer would be. He wrote poems for her, naming them "Elsa's eyes" and "To my beloved Elsa." She'd retort, "But I don't mean necklaces that chocked my time and tied up my hands, now forever poised in their arthritic, artificial clasp holding a needle; I mean my novella with the same name. Do you think that it is worth publishing?"

Aragon would not answer: for him, she was neither Russian-Jewish, nor French; there was no such term as a Jewish or German vagina, and when loving her, he was taking her in one hundred percent, her tongue and organs together, not separating *"sobaka"* from *"un chien"*, *"kolodetz"* from *"un puits"*, *"ruzh'e"* from *"un fusil"*. Yet, his seeming indifference drove her mad.

Every day she expected news from Victor in Russia, but the days were as empty and rusty as her metal mailbox. Victor's love didn't help Soviet apparatchiks accept and accolade Elsa's "bourgeois writing"; besides, she was annoyed by his question, "When you die, Elsa, in which language will your last words be?" This was an intrusion into her mouth that she could not handle.

Nights with Aragon were argumentative; her gums bleeding, she rejected his kisses; when he would touch her right breast, she would counter him with a question, "Don't you think that my *Necklaces* are no worse than some of your writing?" He would proceed to the left breast, but she was inconsolable; she demanded recognition not only in bed but in book. His remaining mute during their lovemaking, never commenting on her new writing, drove her to the brink.

6

MARGARITA MEKLINA

She still had a hard time adjusting to the U.S. after arriving here from Russia fifteen years earlier, sending back her short stories which kept winning prizes in Moscow—Ethan Tanner mailed her the talk on Ukrainian auxiliary police bullets he gave at his office, where he used to catch petrified criminals, views of freshly beautiful women walking by his cubicle on the third floor, or a catnap. He worked on creating a position as a translator for her.

She read line after line, his sexual infatuation with her and his wet, long sentences, almost snail trails, interspersed with dry, awkward quotations in the Ukrainian language from the *L'vivskii* archive: "Our dutiful policemen are impatiently waiting for pistols to start performing the job," "I'm impatiently waiting for the next installment of your confessions, and the more I read about your daily life, your love for bright colors in clothes and brainy men supplying you with intellectual stimulation and supple touches, the more I need to know about you: what time you set your alarm, how many meters from the front entrance you light up your cigarette, how many people you're seeing, how multiple your orgasms might be."

The speed with which she read his e-mails changed according to the time in history: she ran all the red and warning lights in his ramblings about her looks (she was a dark-haired, sharp-featured and foxy beauty over thirty), speeding up through his words and getting stuck in the mud of the past, where every fact was a roadblock: "The policemen knew the city like the backs of their hands and as soon as the order to catch and kill Jews was given to them, they descended on the city, advancing from home to home and attic to attic; those were places and streets where they'd played while growing up and they didn't need any maps, rounding up Jews with unbelievable ease". "With these spare and sporadic letters you sent me, I drew a map of your movements from home to work and from work back home using the fountain pen given to me by my father a long time ago; I know the exact time you arrive and the exact time you go to bed." "Officers of the Third Reich loved their pens, using them for reports, and they carefully listed each one seized from the victims. I'm writing you this letter with a gold nib, which nibbles over each thought I send you."

A much older Ethan, in a ripe marriage that grew sour after ten years, knew Russian and Ukrainian perfectly, spending years in the Soviet and later Finnish archives (each of them came not only with proof of Nazi crimes, but with a new lover who'd help him to unearth them and translate them into an appropriate language; later the name of each police guard was firmly paired in his memory with the name of a girl who provided him with historical facts and sexual favors (or, like he wrote to Margarita, with a smiling emoticon, "erotic flavors and sexual facts about herself and historical favors").

Each document he would send her made her feel closer to her maternal relatives killed in Ukraine in a decrepit ravine: she was half-Jewish, and he was half-joking, she hoped, when telling her about his fantasies. When she would fail to respond, he would force a new suggestion on her, "Why should it be that you are on the sunny West Coast and I'm on the sexless East Coast; couldn't we meet in between?" Knowing she cared about the research that he did at his office, he would attach a report to his letter: "These five Jews were on the roof and I was below, they would not come down and I would not dare climb up to get them, so I simply shot at the roof and all of them fell."

"Liebe M., if you ask me what the Shoah was about, I would tell you that it's about the total obliteration of physical being. I'm looking at myself in the mirror: the skin on my arms is rough and patchy because of my work in the garden under the sun. I would not want to die, be reduced to vapor or carbon, without you returning my affection. At least this way, if I were desired by you, when I died, I would not simply be transformed into some basic elements like Holocaust victims, I would be kept in your beautiful writing in Russian; please call me today and utter some simple words in your Slavic accent, *sobaka* or *seksapilnost'*, whatever words come to your mind. Please do it today at 10 p.m., right before I go to bed."

"Liebe M., when giving my talk yesterday at 'Jewish Justice', I informed my listeners about the atomization of 1.7 million bodies that occurred in an area totaling three acres and took about 10 months. Not being able to raise my head from these damn papers describing destruction, I simply want somebody to give me a hug and I would appreciate it if you could finally use your "Razor" at 10:30 p.m. when I will be in bed setting my alarm for tomorrow and thinking of you. If you are afraid of live conversation, please call and leave several words on my recorder: *ia hochu, ia zhelaiu, I goriu zhazhdoi*; I wouldn't pick up, but later I will play the message numerous times."

"Liebe M., your silence throws me into despair: like those Jews who were not allowed even to take up space in the ground, reduced to small fragments of charred material, I'm not allowed into your life and reduced to five letters E-T-H-A-N in your Google mailbox. I know that I'm nothing for you. Please call me today at 11 p.m. before I go to bed and simply pronounce my name."

"Liebe M.: all the nameless Jews killed by the Auxiliary police and SS officers left us no evidence that they'd ever walked the earth, when there was no loved one who'd survived them. I want to be desired by you so that my existence is properly recorded in your precious prose in Russian. Please phone me today evening and let me know that I'm still alive."

After reading his letters, Margarita felt a very strange emptiness which grew in her heart. For several weeks, processing this new information raining down on her in the form of image *gif* files that he'd made from reports by the police in Ukraine in 1942, who with perfect handwriting described the usage of bullets, she retreated, growing more mute than she usually was. Her main interest, apart from answering phones at her dull job, became browsing mail-order catalogs with descriptions of clothes: sweaters and suspenders "maroon," "color of the sunrise," or "burnt orange," coverlets—"peaceful white" and "icy green," turtlenecks—"aquamarine" or "bloody red." This was all of the English, being a Russian writer, she wanted to know.

Like Zinaida and Elsa, uprooted from any feelings of comfort, agonizing and analyzing, unnerved and unsettled, she jumped to her death in an alien tongue.

Numbers

I

Olga's body was found today. Brick homes stand shoulder to shoulder, a square playground is still in its place, with men walking its perimeter in checkered vests, while spewing loud statements about politics, and women quietly reciting recipes and the rising price of milk: nothing has changed, except that the body had been removed from the children's playground, less than one hour after it fell.

It's strange how quickly it was stumbled upon, how efficient my neighbors could be.

When she was alive, they stopped greeting her; they used to pass her on the stairwell or in the street staring straight ahead, pretending she was a speckle of light or a shadow; they already turned her into a shadow, before she actually became one, after jumping from the seventh floor balcony where, in better times, she sat with a promisingly voluptuous volume, this or that full-bodied book.

She told me once, "When I was a child, I didn't know bookmarks existed and I couldn't read either, so I would spend the whole day memorizing the page number where we stopped… In the evening I would recite it to Mamma so that she could read me an entire fairy tale without missing a beat… A page number, I would spend the whole day with only this on my mind."

Olga lived two floors up from me; a lean, dry woman with an unsure posture and a slight bend forward, as though as she was a leaning Tower of Pisa, the woman with a narrow face and pointed nose, as pointed as the tips of her beige shoes, always polished. Her face looked like a black-and-white etching: so clear and straightforward her features were. As years passed, she seemed to appear leaner and more leaning forward, or was this the only detail about her that stuck in my memory?

The neighbors were quick to change their mood toward her, relying not on their feelings (who knows whether they even had any feelings for her; she was lean as a leaflet and passed by as lightly as a leaf carried by the wind), but on something they heard on state radio or glanced in a newspaper, and they were quick, perhaps even too quick, to pick her up when she fell, with the only difference that at this point she didn't care about their efficiency—she was dreadfully dead.

Why this rush? Were they ashamed?

Shame in Italy is associated with silence: nobody mentions Olga these days.

I think that if she fell on the street, because her old legs didn't support her, then it would be a nice thing to do, to come to the old lady and to help her stand up. But now, how can anybody lift her so that she stands up? Or, can she stand up on these pages, depicted by me with such vividness and virtuosity that her blood flows back to her limbs and her veins pulse? It's a rhetorical question. It's the writer in me scorching and making comical and clever faces, when there can be nothing funny or clever.

But back to the neighbors whose collective face is as formless and pasty as dough; they crowd these pages ominously, but they have no distinctive features. They are as noisy as the background of history.

Just a couple of months ago they were looking up to her, a well-dressed, color-coordinated niece of famous publishers, who was married to a well-known realist painter Ferrara.

Ferrara painted striped bathers, strippers and opium smokers in a harem, and he took his wife to an estate on lustrous Lago Maggiore, where they would spend shiny summers. He would grab a wooden foldable easel and stroll to a green hill, and she would take a wooden folding chair and read next to him while he painted. He was a person who found these simple folks unique and worth artistic attention.

In the past, neighbors would say, "Come sta, Signora Olga?" to her, and they would encourage youngsters to approach La Signora and ask how she felt today and what she was up to.

"What do you advise reading, Signora Olga? My Giovanni is ten and behind his classmates. We want him to read, but not become as well-learned as you are; that is too much; we want him to be a man of trade; reading is just something he can do when he is tired after helping his father in the workshop." Or: "How were you able to make your plant stand upright on your balcony? It's gangly and tall but it does not break." Or: "Signora Olga, you are always reading… why don't you go on a picnic with us? Or just by yourself? Your eyes are bloodshot."

They were awkward in their questions, but they didn't need answers; they thought it was required of them to make small talk to bridge the silence and social gaps between them, a gap between her refined restraint and their loose folksy manners. My neighbors are simple people, and in Northern Italy simple people still respect knowledge and admire complexity. Yes, they still do.

When I would tell a butcher next door that I am a writer in the making, he would summarize for me the plot of the recent crime novel he had read (the plot as ghastly as the meat that he sold, leaving blood stains on his white apron), and then he'd wink and look up, as though peering through an imaginary hole into Olga's apartment, and would say something like: "Those Scarfati were dirt poor when they arrived here from France a hundred years ago, and now they are so full of themselves they won't even talk to a butcher… They publish books, plain books with numbered pages in which I sometimes wrap meat, tenderloin on page five, ribs on page two hundred three, and they got a special talent for turning these books into homes and villas. Look at them: they have healthy complexions, and their children eat quality meat, not the stuff I sell to weathered widows who can only afford big bones with their crinkled small bills; these Scarfati are quite a success,"—and he would laugh, and his huge belly would move, so that I would feel rather repulsed and even nauseated and not sure anymore of why I again started talking to him. Maybe because of my loneliness? I have no friends and no foes, and sometimes I'm so absorbed in reading and writing that I forget to turn the calendar page…

Recently the butcher, when I ran into him outside an elevator, asked me, "How come you never visit my store? You never bought my pork! And you never played with my daughters! Something's wrong with you, isn't it? You are not like everybody else, right?," and I felt that there was something else he wanted to utter, but he hesitated and didn't say the full truth of what was on his primitive, meaty mind.

I hesitated to tell him that I didn't buy meat from him because I have a very delicate stomach and I don't eat meat, since it makes me feel sick. I just stood mute and stared at him trying to see whether there was anything hidden behind these harsh words, and, apparently ashamed by his blatant outburst, he suddenly mumbled: "Never mind, Rita!" Then added: "Listen, if you have problems, just let me know—I'm not such a beast as you imagine me to be, and I can even be useful to you,"—and I realized that maybe he indeed had a hidden door in him, which would lead me past his fatty and ugly appearance to some well-hidden precious spot.

"I can hide you in my shop when the time comes,"—he uttered, and I shivered because the word on my mind—"hidden"—coincided with this uttered word. The word "hide," apparently, was becoming important.

Later I noticed that neighbors stopped saying *buon giorno* to me, as though they were trying to turn me into Olga Ferrara. How were they able to sense that I was like her? Was it truly because of me being part-Jewish, or was it because of this "air of superiority" that I have, according to my father's impression of me? I am fair-skinned and my hair is not at all curly, as Jews are depicted in caricatures in Fascist newspapers, and if something stands out in the crowd, it's my somewhat arrogant look. Papá laughs at me saying that this is because I read too much philosophy, but when he checked my eyesight, he realized that it was because of my far-sightedness, a trait shared by him. I never thought of myself as anything but Italian, but apparently nationality is becoming crucial—just as the word "hide."

Yet, literature is above all: above skin color and a particular local language, and that's why I have been focusing on my craft instead of a cranium's shape. There is no way circumstances will prompt me to jump from the fifth floor, because, as a writer, I have a lot to say to the world. Because of this talent, I have to preserve myself no matter what blood runs in my veins.

II

As an aspiring writer trying to spring onto my feet, I knew that it was not by chance that I lived only two floors down from Olga, the niece of the prominent publishers.

Her uncles owned the publishing house "Fratelli Scarfati" which not only took under its wide wing Edmondo de Amicis and Gabriele D'Annunzio, and just about every revered Italian man and woman of letters, but also wined and dined them and threw them lavish literary parties. For me, such proximity was like a sign, an arrow showing me the right path.

I thought that this was the way for a writer: to be published by a well-respected publishing house like Fratelli Scarfati and then to be able to buy villas and vineyards and see how words turn into material wealth.

Every time I would spot Olga sitting outside on a bench with a leathery book with gold embossing, I would ask, "Another Fratelli Scarfati production?" And she would nod, "Yes, this is an avant-gardist Marinetti," or "Yes, Fratelli Scarfati published this novel by Pirandello, and this is the second edition, because the first was so popular that it got sold out within one month!" I liked repeating the words "Fratelli Scarfati," because it made me feel close to them: I am an unknown, but already know somebody from the majestic and mysterious literary world.

After Olga's death, this golden glorious feeling

deserted me. Is her suicide a sign for me, too? Maybe, I should write a story about the days preceding her death, but first I would have to find memorable details about this suicide, something that makes it unlike all the others.

My favorite writer, a Russian named Chekhov, routinely paid attention to the smallest detail, and one of his heroes would get into a funny pose (raising his right hand and his left leg, as though in an absurd ballet) and say funny words, and another would fall out of love just because his beloved was writing bad romance novels... What if I had ended up living in Olga's proximity not because that closeness brought to my consciousness the luxuries promised by literature, but because I was destined to find something special in Olga's life, which would reveal our times?

But a body... the dead body—how memorable or special can it be by itself, if you don't describe the wedding ring of her late husband that she was wearing on her finger, a ring so big that she attached it to her own with a yellow thread so it would not slip off... I don't remember meeting him, being an infant when he succumbed to an illness, but I heard that besides being a painter, he was an inventor and that they were deeply in love... I could describe how a neighbor, hoping that nobody saw him, pulled both rings from Olga's finger so fast that they got stuck and, while doing so, removed some skin from her already dead finger... Did this really happen? I don't know; I didn't see. But those details are the ones that make literature real, and I have to practice every day to be able to spot them.

At this point, the time has come to show my face, which I have been successfully hiding behind the story of death. A writer has to interest readers, the readers who have no inclination to philosophize, or to question whether there is Judgment Day or humanity; the reader has to get all the gory or glorious details up front. You don't hook fish with abstractions, my father taught me; you throw bait, and this bait would be me.

I'm lucky, because, with my looks, I could easily pass for a heroine of a novel. Whichever I choose: I can be a writer, or a hero of a story, or both if necessary. Perhaps, I shall make myself a major heroine of this story, even though I have no idea where it will lead me. I only know that I have to write every day to be rid of my fear of emptiness, when no words come from the pen, despite my home's conveniences and my mental convulsions…

I was born twenty-two years ago, in a doctor's family, and my mother, who was not so happy with her housewife status and stale, unrevivable bread and expiring youth, left when I was seven. She ran away with an émigré, an affable cavalry officer whom the Russian Revolution had left without a home or hopes of coming back, and I do not know where they went, but five years ago my father received a letter with Australian stamps and, upon receiving it, he closed the door to his room with a faint smile, but when he emerged, he was averting his eyes. I don't know whether my mother still lives with kangaroos and that officer in Australia or she abandoned him the same way she jettisoned my Papá; I only know that it's prohibited in our home to speak her name, as though she were God who abandoned us.

My father is a doctor and he is Jewish; my mother is half-French, half-Italian, and I'm supposed to be part-French too, even though I was "part-French" only for seven years and after those seven years I spent with her, I'm not convinced that I need to share with her anything else, including nationality.

Almost up to this day, I studied chemistry, because two of my uncles studied chemistry too, and they said that you always could find a job as a pharmacist, so I was going to a university, despite the fact that all I wanted was to practice writing instead of writing chemical formulas that—if you drop water on a page of a notebook—smear and disappear into a dirty cloud as fast as though dissolved by chlorine. Now they have said that a university is no place for Jews, so I was happy that I could devote all my time to literature instead of the Periodic Table or mixing concoctions in a nondescript glass.

I am tall and thin and I look like one of the actresses in silent movies, which means that I don't even have to open my mouth to be expressive; it's my large, dark eyes accentuated by brownish shades under them that express everything (because of my face structure, my high cheekbones, and my inability to eat meat). I have long hair that I keep in braids, and my dresses fall slightly below the knee. The only minor problem is that I limp when I walk, because I was born with one leg shorter (and my mother was too, which didn't prevent her from running, with her affable officer, very fast and away from her *cara famiglia*), and I always have to put a special platform under my heel.

But when I'm a published author, my legs won't matter, because on books, they publish faces: of foxy women in hats and of men with cigars or with guns or pens, something elongated and firm which remind us of masculinity. My limp will look good in my biography though, making me special. I'm here to write down everything. To observe and report. I'm here to imbibe all the dreadful details of everyday life and turn them into beautiful fiction.

Yes, I would like to write fiction; the only thing I don't want is to become a fact or a casualty. I will survive this difficult period exactly because I have this talent for writing, and it cannot be that it's given to me by God just to waste. It's here for a purpose and as long as I continue writing, I'll continue living.

III

After you have seen my curious, elongated, dark face with long braids in the mirror of your imagination, after you have felt sorry for my shorter left leg and lusted after my youth and then scorned me for my boastfulness and naiveté, I'll get back to Olga Ferrara.

Three months ago I met her on the street: she was dressed in a bright maroon dress and an elegant hat, nothing similar to that dark, ugly, drab outfit in which she was found lying on the playground—isn't it strange to think that, despite this bleak outfit, she was discovered and then her body disposed of so quickly, as though the neighbors had been prepared to promptly help her say good-bye to this world.

There are rumors that she left a note which was found on her body and later disposed of, together with it, as though both her words and flesh were dangerous, and in this note she said that she was ending her life, because she could not bear the shame and burden of racial laws which looked upon her as a second class person. She said that she had been living in terror for several years, hoping that eventually somebody with a clear mind would once and for all tell the others that what they are doing and thinking about Jews was sheer madness, but nobody even tried to shake off this nightmare, and now life had just turned into crude darkness.

She could not believe that humanity had came to this, and she mentioned that she was scared, simply scared of continuing to live in such a world, being a person who didn't deserve scorn and shame, being the niece of famous publishers who were bringing humanity and enlightenment by publishing the luminaries of their time. These luminaries, according to her words, cared about simple folk, describing simple folk with sympathy and understanding, the same way her husband Ferrara painted seamstresses and bakers, red-cheeked wet nurses and thick-thighed laundry women drying their hands, instead of glorifying only his class.

Before the racial laws, Olga was first class, refined and educated, and now she was second and perhaps even third, despised and unwanted. But now, in the afterlife, which class had she become?

Maybe she indeed wrote all those things in her final note or maybe she didn't, or, perhaps, she said it in other words totally unlike mine—I will never know, because one of the neighbors whispered to me that the note had been buried together with Olga, and now nobody will ever know her last words. There was no obituary in the newspaper, because the racial laws prohibited publishing "Jewish" obituaries, and this was like spitting in her face: all her life she loved words and reading, and after her death she was denied even a handful of words published about herself.

When I met her three months ago, she was still smiling and, upon hearing that I was trying to write every day and that I admired her uncles who socialized with the luminaries of their time, publishing Luigi Pirandello and Giovanni Verga, and Edmondo de Amicis among many others—upon hearing this, she led me to her apartment and produced a large album that those Italian intellectuals—including my favorite, Marinetti—signed for her uncles. She led me to her apartment and she served me a cup of tea with *lingue di gatto*, and then she opened a cupboard, and gave me this heavy album that was published in celebration of the fiftieth anniversary of the "Fratelli Scarfati Publishing House." And I read, one by one, commentaries left by writers who expressed their thankfulness to the Scarfati: for supporting their talents, for paying for their words, for publishing their work, for making their word and world known and heard.

I think I should write a short story about Olga; I just need to find a detail that will be so memorable that her face will stand out before the reader, but I just don't know what to describe besides her black outfit hardly visible on the playground, masked by green and lush foliage... what details should I emphasize?

How she saw a caricature in a newspaper which depicted a red-nosed Jew selling used razors—a huge caricature figure putting that razor almost to the throat of a poor Italian worker—and suddenly, after living for several years under this burden, realized that she could stand it no more? I'm really at a loss for words. All I can repeat is her name, Olga. Why did her parents give her such a Russian name? Was there any meaning behind it?

I have no colorful details in mind, only her name: Olga, Olga, that's what I repeat at nights when I fall asleep, I repeat her name "Olga," and hope that the God of inspiration will bring some idea to my mind overnight... I repeat "Olga, Olga," and I start crying, and I think that my name is Rita and it's a typical Italian name, it's not Russian, and I know that Rita must survive these difficult times despite the fact that Olga is dead.

IV

Words come from emptiness now.

Before they were coming from inside myself, living in an apartment full of old furniture: a cherished cherry bouillotte table where my father would lay out the cards and explain to me the difference between the King and the Jack; a large wardrobe inherited from my mother's ancestors; a jewelry chest where I loved to put my little fingers, hoping that it held treasures and only finding lonely earrings and brooches with crooked clasps left by my mother who had run from our home in haste.

Each day I would sit with an ink pen in one hand and touch an ink well with the other, as though trying to ignite words with this friction, and I would describe furniture in details, and it would lead me to stories.

What about that trunk? It has a story. Full of patriotism, my father wanted to fight in the Great War and promptly signed up, rented a little room in a Naples hotel and decided to make his last day before military service distinct and full of action. He spent all his money in an upscale restaurant ordering as many *moscardini* dishes as he could, because he couldn't imagine his life without his *moscardini*, and while he was enjoying his dinner, a young girl approached him and somehow, awkwardly positioning and repositioning their elbows through the artillery of plates to touch each other's hands, they became friends.

He paid for her meal too and got drunk, not noticing that she was totally sober. With a concerned look on her face, she told him that she wanted to make sure that he was okay and she would help him walk to his hotel. They got out of the restaurant under the ironic glances of the owner and two gaunt waiters; he didn't notice these glances in his nauseous intoxication, but she was used to them and therefore unflappable. When he woke up, he remembered that he had been trying to lie down in bed and she had assisted his every movement, but he was not sure whether he had become a man that night. He felt embarrassed, because he didn't remember what had happened, but he saw a stocking that she left by mistake or as a somewhat sadistic or sardonic "hello" from her.

The second reason he was ashamed was that he had overslept and missed a ship that all his new friends had boarded for Macedonia to fight the war. My father told me that he woke up totally disheveled and with a bitter taste in his mouth no longer reminiscent of *moscardini*, and immediately noticed that the girl had stolen even a family portrait in a silver frame that he'd left standing on the side table, and this realization was painful, because he had thought her to be honest and was hoping that she would wait for him while he was fighting in the war.

Both with this prostitute and later with my mother, my father was very naïve.

When he ran to the pier, he saw his boat leaving, and no matter how hectically he jumped on the shore with his suitcase filled with underwear necessities and a supply of ink to write letters home to Mamma and Papá (the ink wells and pens made a funny sound jumping up and down with him inside his cardboard suitcase, the suitcase of his poorer *commicitone* to whom he gave his leather one), no matter how many people he approached asking for assistance—bureaucratic or hands-on and practical—nobody could help to erase this ever-increasing distance between him and the ship; the distance between him and his death, because the ship was bombed by the enemy and went down taking with it all the would-be heroes, as my father learned later from the newspapers.

Or what about the telegram?

This framed telegram was from the Russian physiologist Ivan Pavlov who was fascinated by the work of the Italian physiologist Angelo Rosso. Angelo Rosso researched what mountaineers experienced in high altitude, and he also invented a device which would determine, by how your blood pulsed and your heart pounded, whether you were lying or telling the truth, and his published findings were later translated into multiple languages including Russian. When the Russian physiologist heard of his Italian colleague's death, he promptly sent a telegram to Rosso's relatives with condolences, and then this telegram was framed and stood for a long time in Olga's home, because Angelo Rosso was married to her sister Mimí.

When I entered Olga's apartment after her death, partially for memories, partially for my research, to determine what is left of a person who has departed this world forever, I saw that the neighbors had already carried everything out. But they took only parts of Olga's story and the story will never be complete, since her things will lose their voice in strangers' hands.

The belongings from Olga's apartment, a wardrobe or a trunk, will have no meaning to the neighbors, because who in their right mind would say to their growing kids: "We killed Olga with silence and passivity when anti-Semitic drawings started appearing in print and then spilled from the pages, and then we took not only her life but her belongings as well?" No, these things will be just things, useless things without words behind them. The only piece of remembrance left for me in that ransacked apartment was this telegram, and this telegram has words from the famous Russian scientist, words that meant nothing to my uneducated neighbors, who still valued knowledge and respected educated people, but only when it was convenient and sanctioned by newspapers; when newspapers said that Jews were second class, it became so in these people's minds.

I'm sitting in emptiness and, only with my memory,

with a familiar feeling, I'm entering my former flat.

I see marks on the door frame, where my father checked, with a pencil, how tall I was; I see my books on the shelf, the books that my father forbade me to read in a bathroom or next to a plate with *risotto*; I see a painting on the wall, with fruits in a basket and a duck with a long neck, whose head is hanging very low from the table (I always thought this too brutal, but father said it was by a famous painter); I also see ceramic bowls my father collected, each piece means something only for me.

If we put all these bowls in one large room, collected from each person living in our home, they will lose all the words behind them. If we collect all the jewelry from people's homes and fill all these bowls, it will be only a shiny material with no depth, cold gold without emotions.

Without being able to enter my apartment these days, I can recreate it from memory and, if I write about it by simply naming the objects, the story will make sense only to somebody who lived in a similar flat, in a similar situation, in the same town, whose things, like mine, were taken from them. They were placed in a strange train crammed together as closely as sardines in a can and yet never becoming truly close, only physically, but never emotionally, and on that train, all they have are memories of their apartments, and all I have besides this is the memory of my father who had disappeared.

Together with a few necessities, I was able to sneak in pencils and notebooks, and I force myself to write, and I try to be oblivious to the misery and awful things around me, because I have to focus on literature, and I believe that since I was given this gift as a writer—a gift even more individual and intensely personal than objects with stories behind them—I will survive as long as I write.

V

I was born twenty-two years ago, and, from an early age, I knew that a large destiny awaited me.

From a very early age, I was interested in book reading, even my father's books that were medical encyclopedias with skeletons and veins and awful ruptures of the body depicted on its colorful pages. When I was five years old and he taught me how to write, I immediately wrote a letter to my mother in my childish scrawl, and since my mother at the time was still with us (but already planned, through an underground tunnel of her soul, to escape), she was touched.

The letter said the following: "My dear mother… yesterday you had a headache… do you feel better? Feel better, papa and me love you." It was not grammatically correct, not at all, but these were simple words and they touched a spot in my mother's soul, and when she ran away, she apparently took with her that letter and also my photo.

When I was eleven, I made my own "book" by putting together, with a needle and bright red thread, notebook pages. The story—illustrated by nothing other than snow—was about two snowmen who lived in their own kingdom. When I turned fifteen, my father was asked to write articles for a magazine covering the history of pharmacology, and I helped to edit those articles we composed together while laughing and making fun of future readers who would seriously read what we wrote in such a funny manner, between supper and falling asleep.

Among those articles were a vignette about Tibetan medicine, and a book of medical potions penned by the Arab doctor Al Beruni, and about medications useful for treating oneself against dog's madness. My love for the written word was so strong that I enjoyed even helping my father to write these articles, not only fiction. Thinking of my father, I cannot forget his face when he was saying the last good bye to me a month ago…

It's true that I try only to focus on writing, because I have a strong feeling that if I continue writing, I will survive these dreadful times. Writing is why I was brought to this world in the first place, otherwise why such an urge to hold a pen from such an early age? Why such an urge to document everything and to remember every little detail, as though for posterity? This is something beyond and above me, something I was given for free but something that I have to repay since it always forced me to action. Every time there was a movement inside me because I saw something unusual, this movement would propel me to paper, but things that recently started happening in my life are so incomprehensible that I'm not sure that I can find an explanation, that I can frame these events and hang them on the wall of my short story. What's happening is so big and so imposing that I'm not yet skillful enough to describe it.

Should I describe my father's eyes behind his thick-lensed glasses when he was looking at me saying *arrivederci*? He told me that we'll meet again soon, while being led away by two policemen; my father was always smart and before this day he kept telling me that this might happen, but I never could understand why, if he knew that somebody would come after him, he didn't do anything to escape. And could we go somewhere else? We have a faraway relative in Switzerland, and we could try to cross the border and reach comparable safety, but for some reason we never did. Before this, one of the passersby, a petite man, whom I would not even have noticed if he hadn't stopped me, in a grey threadbare coat and with hair of indistinguishable color, made a little gesture while walking toward me on the street.

He gestured at me to stop and to go to the side of the sidewalk, to the steps of a caffé where my father always urged me to stand while drinking coffee instead of sitting, because drinking coffee while standing costs slightly less… This man motioned me to the side and told me, "Signorina, once you father treated my wife for free, when she was very sick, my wife died anyway, but it does not matter right now… I know him to be a good man, and I want to warn you that I know that they will come to your flat soon and take him away; whatever you want to do to escape this situation, do it, but don't tell anybody that I have told you this, understand?" I'm rather awkward in conversations, and he was too, so we both said several times "thank you" to each other and immediately separated, as though even standing on the street together, sharing the same knowledge, was very risky.

I told Papá about this man, and he could not remember who it was, despite my descriptions of a gray coat and indistinguishable grayish hair; my father just kept repeating, "There were so many of them, these poor Italian peasants, all saying that they have no money to pay for medical services, and there were so many that I helped for free and so many that I could not help for any amount of money, that I do not remember this noble gentleman, and he indeed seems noble, despite his apparently peasant upbringing… but where will we go, Rita? Do you think there is a way to escape? Why not stay in our nice apartment, in relative safety, and hope that the danger will pass by itself? Besides, you didn't do anything bad, and you are such a nice girl, whoever will look at you will see no danger in you, and maybe nobody will ever find out about your Jewish blood... It's in Australia that you will be safe, with your mother and her Russian officer... but who will let us go to Australia? Maybe you can try to write to your mother and see if she can do something for you..."

And so he spoke and so he stayed in the apartment, and so he was led away and they didn't take me; for some reason that happened later. And now, sitting on this wretched train going somewhere with a slow yet steady speed, I don't know how to describe all that is happening. If I describe my father's tears and his hat that fell from his head, the hat he didn't even bother to pick up, and if I describe his shoes, or a book that he tried to take with him, under the ignorant eyes of the policeman, would it be enough for the story? My father's nervous voice and his worry for me...

Does it make any sense, these little details described by a skillful craftsman of words, who only sees these details, but does not know what caused them? What is the overall plan? Who needed for Olga to jump from the balcony, my father to be led away from me for no reason, and for me to stay, with my talent for words, now unable to open my mouth?

I know that my only value is my talent with words... If I don't practice it and don't hone it to become a writer like those published by Fratelli Scarfati, then I will be like everybody else; I know that if I don't have my own very special words to speak to readers whom I will never meet, then I will share everybody else's fate and will be doomed.

So, despite being on this ugly train where we are unfed, stripped of privacy, and have no chance to bathe, where we are denied not only every kind of pleasures but every kind of basic conveniences, I'm saving my spirits and distracting myself from reality by trying to write and finally find an artful detail that will make sense, will reveal something of an overall design, and will turn this design into an elegant story.

VI

I have been unusually silent these last two days. I still keep guarding a couple of notebooks and a whole box of sharpened pencils that I was able to take with me… however, I only write down my thoughts, which is not art… my own thoughts would only be interesting for my biographers when I become famous… or for a researcher studying the racial laws and the War… but the literary world needs something beautiful and miraculous, perhaps a novel or a couple of them, something for which I know I was born and kept alive—fate always protected me—but I seem incapable of producing anything nowadays…

It's as though together with my possessions and family flat (perhaps now occupied by the greedy butcher with his meat bricks and daughters looking like meat bricks, too, square and red), they took from me the ability to describe things…

But should I describe things I see in front of myself… what kind of literature would it be if I describe today's fight for a piece of paper that another woman on the train wanted to take from me to cover her excrements? I can't even say this—so unpoetic and totally ridiculous this is… but yes, this is what happened today. Once the train stopped in the middle of the field, among some grass and weeds, and we were allowed to jump down and to do whatever we needed to do, people decided that there would be more such stops, each with more and more conveniences… Everybody on the train was thinking that we were going somewhere to the East to work and to be useful, so we were expecting not this grass or weeds; we were expecting at least some rooms with basics like a floor, a door, or a window with a curtain…. That's why when the train stopped and some men went to the left and some women to the opposite direction to take care of their bodily needs, some people said, "Well, we'll wait till we come where they are taking us; here it's not the best place."

This woman, she was always staring at me when I was trying to write… she almost was giving me this dirty look, not understanding that the time of dirty looks had passed together with the peace and quiet… now nobody cares about her demanding and angry glances… she was older than me, in a dark coat and a dark scarf on her head blending her into the dark innards of the train…and she was staring at me as though it was no time for writing now… and then she said, "Why won't you give me a couple of pages from your sketchbook?" And I asked her, "But I need them myself, why are you interested?" And she said that she had to have them to cover some dirt… she didn't mind explaining it to me in her dialect… When I said "No," she got very mad. She said that she needed it for "a real thing," not "philosophical thoughts."

She said to me literally the following:

—Who do you think you are? Do you think you can work for Germans better than me simply because you have good handwriting? Don't hope! They'll kill you together with me. And I'm not as educated as you are. I earned my living with my hands…

And she showed me her calloused hands; they were not as ugly as one might think at first… actually, she had long beautiful fingers…

Despite her nice hands, her mouth was ugly. She kept repeating:

—You all will die here! You all will die!

And people were turning their eyes away from her, and then one man shouted at her, "Shut up or we'll strangle you, so you'll die because of us Italians and not because of the Germans if you don't keep silent."

And only after the shouts did she stop saying nonsense. But she kept whispering in my direction:

—Don't think that your pen will be useful to you in the hell where we're all going!

I'm not sure whether I was annoyed or not by this; rather, I wanted to protect my pencils and paper and, also, I wanted to watch this woman very carefully to see whether she could become a character in my story, but, again, besides her calloused though aristocratically shaped hands, I didn't find any detail worthy of literature, and I kept silent.

It has been a couple of days since I talked to anybody; I don't eat and I don't feel hungry, even though other people on the train are stealing things from each other and fight for each crumb... but what really bothers me is that I don't write anymore.

I'm even happy now that life provides me no conveniences for writing, with almost no light in these cars, but instead gives me excuses... Whom am I trying to fool? Writing is survival for me. Despite what this woman said, I'm protected by my talent... so much talent cannot be wasted, and to earn my right to live, I have to utilize my creative abilities, so in the next few days I have to come up with a story, otherwise, I will die.

VII

Loneliness on the train... crowds of strangers... surrounded by them, I feel even lonelier, because somebody chose all these people thinking of them as one kind, but I'm of a totally different kind. I'm not interested in trite things and conventional wisdom; neither did I take with me family gold, like some people did. One of the guys here is hiding a miniature Torah in a large loaf of bread, but none of them would care about Fratelli Scarfati or fame.

Days are turning into torture.

And this torture is not because there is almost nothing to eat, a good-looking girl always can find food for herself using her charm… but I'm tortured because I don't know what to make of what is going on.

For example, my father: he was spared by the ship and killed by the bicycle. Is there any logic in this? He missed his ship in the Great War because of alcohol and *moscardini* and he survived… he didn't know how to ride a bike to escape from a concentration camp and so he stayed there…

This is how I found out about it: a man approached me and told me that he was one of my neighbors I hardly knew him but agreed that this could be the case, since I don't pay attention to things not pertaining to literature. The "neighbor" told me that my father was led to the jail in Milan, a big jail where it was cold and icy and people slept on the beds of ice and got sick and died there, but my father survived the prison ordeal, and ended up in an Italian concentration camp, where rules were rather lax; actually, they were so lax that one of the inmates suggested a plan of escape…

This inmate, a former patient whom my father once treated for gall stones, gave my father a hand-drawn map and arranged for a bicycle, so that all my father had to do was to sneak to the fence, climb onto the bicycle seat and pedal toward a village where a Catholic priest already expected him…

But one has to know my Papá… my Papá never rode a bike in his life, he only read books… so he rejected the offer explaining that he was not able to ride a bike… his former patient could not believe this and thought that my father simply didn't want to risk other lives, because if the fascists discovered that one person escaped, they would kill ten… it's all numbers for them… This inmate told me that my father stayed and apparently died, because one day he just went "to work" and he never came back, and this inmate had no idea what happened.

I could not bear to hear this, but after my sadness my brain switched on… here is the story of a man saved by missing a boat, and here he is failed by his inability to ride a bike… the ship saves him but the bicycle is a traitor… Is there logic in this??

Is there any logic in the story of Giuseppe, the story which another neighbor told me?

One morning Giuseppe felt like smoking and realized that there were no cigarettes at home, so, with an old smoker's urgency, he went down to get them, and when he came back only half an hour later, he saw that all his nine children and wife were gone, taken away by the SS. Giuseppe survived, but his wife and nine children were taken in an unknown direction… No logic again!

The story I write should be straightforward…. It should be about numbers, perhaps… I was touched by Olga's story about her childhood and the page number she had to keep in her memory to report to her mother… and I thought that to base a short story on that would be nice… not numbers referring to the extermination of ten people for the escape of one person, but numbers referring to pages of literature… as soon as I find something logical and conclusive, I will start and complete my masterpiece.

The only problem is that during these days on the train I wrote almost zero number of words, real "art" words, not just scribbles in a diary; unfortunately, things that I find just don't seem worth mentioning. Stories of bodyselling on the train that goes right in front of my eyes… glimpses into physical pleasure when you start eating… constant quarrels over the lack of conveniences…. Overall, I just don't feel like writing, it's like some kind of writers' block prohibits such descriptions… or maybe I see some truth here, some deep meaning of whatever is happening to all of us, to all Italian Jews, and I just don't want to confess it. And because of it, because I don't want to utter this truth, because of it I don't write? This is what I heard happens to writers who cease writing once and forever: they suddenly discover the truth, but are so afraid of uttering it—uttering it would be like accepting its existence—that they stop writing.

Looks like lately I have been suffering from this well-known condition. But there is a slight difference: in my situation, if I write, I continue living, because I have nothing left on this train except my writing abilities, and my faith in my talent keeps me alive.

VIII

Hours pass, and no words come from me. Kilometers pass outside the train's window, and I cannot come up with any phrases. Days pass, and I still have not shaped a story idea in my mind. One person died on the train, but they quickly got rid of her, she was very old. There was no way to bury her and no way to continue going on with the dead body, so they just threw her out of the train, so fast that I didn't even have time to take a look…

My neighbor, the woman who was begging me for paper, became my good friend here. She does not ask me for paper anymore, and I don't frown when she attends to her bodily needs right in the crowded passenger carriage; everybody seems to get used to such things. So, this woman told me that the elderly train "passenger" had a weak heart, and it appears that hours on the train weakened her even more, and she passed away.

This elderly woman was very quiet so I never paid any attention to her; there were no special details either in her clothes or her appearance, so I never got inspired to include her in my future fiction… I'm thinking of this all the time now: there are so many of us here on the train, we have lost our individuality;

we have become a collective body: hungry, unkempt, unashamed of our bodies, begging for crumbs—there is nothing individual anymore, but art calls for an individual detail about a person… I tried to concentrate on a woman or man and describe him or her, but people became so indistinguishable here, all starving and with bad skin and with a bad smell, that there seems to be no distinction between them… I assume that inside everybody is different, but how can I know that? People here became distrustful, and each has his problems and worries, so everybody is now becoming more silent and just keeps to himself.

That's why in my would-be short story I should stick to Olga. Olga was an individual before she ended her life. She was a niece of famous publishers, and she tried to remember pages in her children's books, she was unique, and now I suspect that this is why her only option was suicide. With fascist racial laws and an overall negative attitude toward Jews encouraged by Nazis, she knew that she was not considered an individual anymore… she was considered a part of an alien population… she had no face and no history, she was only hated as a general body, as a concept, the concept of the "greedy Jew." Her individualistic act of suicide was a protest against losing her own face.

And for me, not to lose my own face and my own individuality, I have to write. I have to write, but I can't force myself. I have gotten crushed in this train, they try to make me nothing, and a nothing obviously cannot have its own thoughts, but it's not only this, it's also that I have become weak, and sometimes I only think of food, my desire for food, any kind of food, a hot potato or hot milk, something I considered too simple during my "other" life before this train.

The people on the train devised a game: they talk about foods their mothers cooked for them in their childhood, and this turns everybody into a hysterical creature. After discussing food, nobody can sleep anymore and everybody lies with their eyes open, and it is as though those hot potatoes and hot milk float in front of them… But for me, maybe, it's only an excuse… it's been days since I last took a pencil in my hands, and I feel that I'm losing my individuality and my only quality that made my life worth living, and I am starting to be afraid that I'm not going to become a writer, because I'm just not strong enough and don't have enough drive…

IX

Today finally the train stopped. We were in the middle of the same nondescript land that surrounded us before, but now this nondescript land was full of meaning. Before it was just nothing, a nameless piece of earth, and now it was a place where our future is waiting for us. People started laughing and smiling. We got out of the train and started walking around stretching our limbs. Hot water and even soup was provided. We were screened, fed and led to barracks. These barracks all looked the same, without any distinguishing details, just wooden homes with some benches and some windows and basic doors, but still it was better than trains. They told us that tomorrow we are going to be washed and groomed, our hair will be cut, and doctors will check who is going to get which jobs.

I was thinking that I cannot do much, and my friend Nina thought that despite her skills with laundering and with cleaning and all kind of domestic work, she wouldn't be useful. She repeated, "I think it's the end; I don't think they need any maids right now here, in the middle of nowhere, they are fighting the war and they need people to build tanks; I can't build tanks, I only can wash clothes and mend them, so I think we'll be exterminated, sooner or later."

I didn't know what to make of this and hesitated to attribute such words to her usual pessimism; I was not looking ahead very much toward any possible job the Germans could offer me, but I was hoping to get a place in an office so that I could work on papers. I have good handwriting, and I know some bookkeeping and I was hoping that while doing this bookkeeping for the Germans, I would be able to have time for writing. I almost felt today that I was on the verge of a new story… I'm almost there despite my desperation yesterday…

The next day they woke up us early, and I was happy to get out of the barracks because I hadn't slept the whole night. There were at least five of us on the wooden bed, and they were only faces for me, again nothing individual, nothing to create a story out of. Besides, they were pushing me trying to get a bigger place on the bench so I even fell once, and I now have a bruise on my back and on my elbow. There are rumors that they are going to tattoo a number on our arms, and I thought that modern life is such that what was a number for Olga, the number of a page in a children's book, now became a number on the arm, a number not inspired by fantasy, but a number to keep people in check, to keep them as a mass without a face.

And here is where the idea for a new story struck me: when they told us all to undress and to go take a shower. They told us the following, "You are all unkempt from riding in a train for so long, so we are going to wash you. We built showers for you there, in that ravine; you are going to be very clean. We are going to take care not only of your body; we are going to take care also of your clothes."

"Oh my,"—said one Italian woman who was helping a German officer. "You look like an intelligent girl but your clothes look so bad," and she looked at me with such grief, that her face reminded me of my mother's face in the picture… she looked at me as though she knew that she was causing me the pain, but still she kept causing it… I couldn't understand why this woman was looking at me with such sadness… we were only going to take a shower in a ravine…

A German officer said, "Tell them to hang their

clothes on these hooks with numbers, and make them write these numbers on their hands so they remember… this way, everybody will come back to their clothes and their clothes won't be lost…"

And then my friend Nina said, "Well, I thought that they were going to kill us here, but if they make us write down the numbers on our palms, it means they really won't do it! Otherwise, if they wanted to kill us, why would they ask us to memorize these numbers or to write them on our hands?"

And I agreed with her. Surely, we'll be safe. I had the idea for the story right at the moment they told us to memorize these numbers on the hooks for our clothes. Nina's number was 8897, and mine was 8816, the one close to her. Nina asked me for a pencil and I gave it to her, and she licked it and from grey it became blue, because it was this special pencil that had ink in it if licked, and she couldn't write this number on her hand because her hands were so callous and so cold, and she asked me to write this number on her hand.

And then I wrote a number on my hand, the number of the hook on which I was supposed to find my clothes when I came back from the shower, clean and ready to complete my story, and now I knew exactly what my story would be. My story would be about numbers, about Olga's pages in a children's book, and these numbers on the hook, the number of hope, when people hope that this number gives them rational meaning and that there is logic in human existence, and that if they have this number, they'll survive because they can return to their clothes after showering, so I realized that my story will be about these numbers and about hope, and there was even some kind of memorable detail worthy of literature: showers in the ravine, showers we didn't see yet, but we envisioned in our hopes to be clean and to return from there, from that strange looking ravine where clean water is waiting for us, and I realized that these hooks on wooden planks with numbers were something really strange, something totally different, something that I could link to the story of Olga and her numbers on the pages of her favorite children books, and now, at this moment, I realized that I will live and that I'll survive these hard times, because my writing talent again was unleashed and because I had in mind the whole story and I was totally ready to complete it once I came back.

The Eighth Day of Hanukkah

"Tonight's the very first night of Hanukkah and Abigail wants you to be present when she lights the candles." Saeed, in his salmon-colored t-shirt with a star-shaped, sharp-edged hole near one armpit, blocked the door. Nina nodded. She'd torn the hole years ago, when he'd prevented her from giving water to their sick toddler. In his native Morocco, they'd wait until the vomiting vanished. In her Motherland, they'd heal children with as many liquids as possible—water and chicken bouillon and fish oil and gooseberry compote— wrap them in blankets and seal the winter windows with cotton balls and tape from the draft. Saeed was impenetrable and as huge as a boulder, always with a plate of a lamb tagine in his hand, so she, overwhelmed by her powerlessness, had just dumped a cup of water on him and shaken him.

Now she held a tea cup again, but this time with vodka. "It's crucial for Abigail." Stocky, meaty, with messy gray hair, imposing, he repeated his words, and she stepped back so that he couldn't smell what she was drinking at seven a.m. His family, Jewish by origin, had split into Muslims and Jews a thousand years ago, and even though he himself was a Muslim, he always displayed a menorah at the counter in his *Mount Zagora, Mediterranean Eatery* and announced to customers that he still cherished his heritage.

"Today I need to be present," Nina decided, driving home with the girls and deliberately not glancing at grocery stores. Her older daughter, a third-grader, had developed some kind of red rash and now sat next to Nina in their beat-up pickup truck reading a Kindle, immersed in digital words, her hair wrapped around her finger, which, in turn, was in her mouth. The younger one, Anya, had just turned two and until half a year ago wore braces to fix her hip dysplasia. Nina still cringed, remembering the pointy, stiff Pavlik harness plastered against her torso and breast and a constant desire to give up breastfeeding and get lost in a bottle. But alcohol would get into the milk.

Today she had to be present so she steered the truck as far away from their undignified, dingy East Oakland FoodMaxx as she could, but suddenly ran into an unexpected speed bump. And then again. Apparently, she'd turned off International too early and inadvertently approached the place she'd been trying to avoid. "I'd better buy some just in case." Unbuckling the kids, bagging the bottles. Waking up only the next morning after the evening of drinking, ashamed.

The second day of Hanukkah, Saeed brought the kids to her work and went straight to *Mount Zagora* where he stayed well after midnight, until the last lonely, greasy, grouchy guest left. "Doesn't Hanukkah involve bread and wine?"—Nina vaguely remembered the gatherings they had had in Russia and asked Abigail to help her find kosher wine on a grocery shelf. At home, she showed her daughter how to strike a match to keep sparks from landing on her skirt—strike it away from yourself. "Your Granddad taught me this. He read you Pushkin's fairy tales when you were five." Abigail's face could not get any redder because of her allergies, but Nina noticed the tears.

"Did I say something wrong?"

"Anya stole my secret box and destroyed the leaves I picked once with Grandfather. Now there's only dry pieces, small brown bits—that's all that's left."

Nina's father—Abigail's Granddad—had had a heart attack on a bus on his 60th birthday. (The driver performing CPR. A straight line on a cardiogram she was given later.) Now she had to finish her drink very fast. (One gulp, then another one. His grave, wet grass, lumps of earth, earth slowly rising to cover the coffin.) That night she again failed to light the candles.

On the third day of Hanukkah she fell asleep after drinking again, and it turned out that although the children lit the candles by themselves, they did not burn the house down, as Saeed expected. "Abigail cried because you weren't with them on such a significant day," he noted sternly. "I'll do my best this evening," Nina answered honestly, and Abigail's face brightened. The pale face of a zombie with red spots under her eyes. A walking mummy. A marble raccoon. "Who's been beating you up?"—her classmates would ask. Nina wondered if Abigail's allergies had gotten worse because she hadn't joined her daughters for the

Hanukkah ceremony. She took a vacuum cleaner and aimed the hose at the corner, hunting for dust. There was a bottle labeled "Electricity" behind the fridge. "I can't miss the lighting today, I simply can't miss it," she swore to herself, then wondered what this bluish "electricity vodka" tasted like. Yesterday she'd wanted to know more about that Straw-ber-Rita from Bud Light. And the day before,—if Chilean wines were better than Argentinean ones. "Stop it," she ordered herself. "Tonight you must be present."

She flipped through the booklet to the description of the Havdalah night, which fell this year on the fourth night of Hanukkah. Made sure there were plenty of matches lying around. Inspected the chipped paint on a menorah, which practical, "no-nonsense" Saeed used to wash in the dishwasher, alongside newly-purchased plates for his restaurant. Read that this night was meant to define the boundaries between the sacred and the everyday. Thanked G-d, "who granted her life, sustained her and enabled her to reach this occasion." Frequently, when drunk, she thought she wouldn't wake up.

Ashamed again, she reached the next morning, having skipped the Havdalah. In the same way, she missed the following three nights. On the eighth day of Hanukkah she made an elaborate dinner for the kids, putting her bottle away, but at the last moment, when Abigail sat little Anya in a high chair with a cookie and apple juice and was ready to open the booklet with the blessings, she couldn't restrain herself and drank up everything. But she still managed to wake up at midnight and get out of bed. The girls, naked, barely covered by a blanket, lay next to each other with their matching plush pups. One by one, she lit all eight candles for them, hesitating to wake them up so late at night to behold the Hanukkah miracle. Learned from Abigail's booklet that ages ago unadulterated, undefiled olive oil with the seal of high priest had been needed for the menorah in the Temple, but only one flask was located with just enough oil for one day. Miraculously, it burned for eight whole days.

Turned the green flask of Jagermeister upside down to get at the last drops and sardonically smiled: her own personal miracle, despite the Hanukkah, had not taken place. For years her regular dose of happiness was an entire 750 ml bottle of liquid. Never less. Often more. Her feverish festive mood—infused by alcohol—could not stretch for eight days like the magical olive oil found by the Maccabees because she could never make her flask last more than one evening.

Professor Ferrara's Flatworms

Professor Ferrara, one of a narrow but passionate circle of scholars who studied flatworms, stroked the side of his dented green car and said: "It's only a scratch!," after which he clarified: "I'm very pleased with it, it doesn't backfire and it runs on electricity." Having covered his guest's suitcase in the trunk with either a stained old sketch-board, or a raincoat that was just as old, and splattered with sloppy and slovenly stains, the professor learnedly remarked: "This is a bad part of town, you've got to keep your eyes and ears open around here," and unhurriedly but dexterously maneuvering his feet, clad in a pair of leather sandals without socks, he walked up to the entrance. He was bald-headed and nimble, his scalp was shiny and his hands and fingernails meticulously clean, and you wanted to be just like him: to walk along the asphalt just as nimbly and unhurriedly and, having been washed by the spring rain, to study the worms that crawl out through the cracks in the pavement. . .

Pascal—who usually wore only black, for the sole reason that he preferred to dress simply, and not at all for the sake of elegance, although he'd been elegant from the day he was born—had run away from his "tyrannical Mediterranean mother" (his expression) to San Francisco before he'd even turned twenty, and had already been working there as a mailman for fifteen years (his mother considered that occupation unbecoming; after all, Pascal's father was an infectious disease specialist), and in the evenings he took classes in linguistics and psychology (his mother didn't like that either: a passing fancy, an American whim, she always said), not so much for educational purposes as to avoid having to spend evenings at home alone, and he'd become acquainted with the professor on the net.

Yet another of Pascal's passions, apart from linguistics and psychology, was the compilation of his family tree—an amateur one, which was growing quite professionally, however, and already numbered six-hundred people, and on one distant branch, obscured by greenery and oblivion, there was situated the worm expert Professor Ferrara. They weren't blood relatives, not in the least; nonetheless, as is always the case in life, the professor exhibited greater interest in that neglected, branchy tree than Pascal's uncle or mother, who couldn't understand why they should concern themselves with the second cousin of their great-grandfather, once removed, who'd distinguished himself by shooting at church bells, or about the grandfather who, in the anxiety-ridden 1920s, had indicated in his passport *libero pensatore*—freethinker—as his religion, and then link them up with little arrows of some kind instead of seeing to it, for instance, that all the members of the family were vaccinated against whatever cold was mowing everybody down that season.

As concerns Ferrara, he not only replied readily, even

too readily, if anything, to the email from his "milk-and-honeyed relative" living in America (swallowing the bait, hook, line and sinker, thought Pascal), but he also sent a person he barely even knew a parcel, which Pascal, a post-office employee in the very department to which it pertained, delivered to himself. The letter was registered, and Pascal-the-mailman signed for it and put it on the porch, under the rug adorned with heavenly blue Warholian flowers, and then all day long, with a sharp pain in his shoulder and the pleasant ache of athletic-like exertion in his work-weary waist, he thought about that padded parcel and how today, instead of going to his linguistics class and blissfully melting away as he scrutinized the tall, slender female lecturer in a black dress and a red neckerchief, who merely accentuated her inconceivable height with a pair of heels (every time she addressed Pascal he would lose his tongue, and it would seem as though he were the one not interested in their further intercourse, rather than she, although actually nobody knew the underlying reason for this), he would position a few more people on his family tree.

Pascal's mother was cold; even the color of her skin—smooth, milky and light—was reminiscent of snow. Her hands were always moistened and smelled of lotion, so that when shaking hands, hers slipped right out of the other person's, whereas Pascal (having been named Pasquale after a Sicilian friend of his parents, but switching in America to just plain Pascal) was swarthy and impulsive, with wavy hair and a scattering of moles on his back, and he would tear up his mother's lily-white letters in a rage, and afterwards, when in place of letters email began to arrive, he would quickly turn off his flat screen as soon as his mother's email knocked against the bottom of his invisible mailbox and up above, cool as her mint candy, he saw the lines: "My dear son, your father's been scheduled for another operation, and as usual you are so far away." And being away from his northern homeland, Pascal found pleasure in the strange convergences that were revealed now and then in the process of studying his family tree...

Alas, when he opened the package he was both disappointed (the tree wasn't going to branch out today) and delighted: before him lay a heavy, bronze coat of arms. It was accompanied by a photograph: Professor Ferrara in the desert, with a rifle at his feet, a turban on his head, and a number of guides, who were evidently members of an indigenous tribe. Both items—the unfamiliar coat of arms, and the photograph with the gratuitous rifle—were valuable precisely because of their worthlessness: after all, the respected university professor had gone to all the trouble of going to the post office and sending them off first thing, which gave the whole thing meaning and authority.

Pascal threw himself into replying by email immediately, but he became enmeshed in a tangle of words: the photo was good because now he could compare the professor visually with his ancestors or recognize him on the railway platform if necessary, but what should he communicate about the rifle and the turban? Why, after thanking him for the parcel he had to say something about the rifle and the coat of arms, so Professor Ferrara would see that Pascal could appreciate all the earth-shattering narrative twists and turns of his romantic life, a life risked in the desert for the pleasure of digging some sort of worms up out of the earth.

Pascal was considerate, polite. The other post-office employees perceived almost every new customer who came to buy stamps or, say, to send oatmeal cookies, blankets or prepaid calling cards off to American soldiers in Iraq as merely the next man or woman with a generic, featureless face in a never-ending, nonrecurring file. But Pascal remembered them all and would often dumbfound some little old lady with a powdered face in a polka-dotted dress with the words: "Yesterday you came in with a yellow umbrella and bought your grandson a blue teddy-bear wearing a mailman's hat," and his memory was impeccably accurate. However, it's unlikely this ability of his was of any use to anybody.

Despite the confused articulation of his thoughts, Pascal felt that he and Ferrara were kith and kin and that he could call or write the professor anytime at all, and the professor would rouse himself and get a move on at once, and together they would begin to water and nurture their tree, and add to the accompanying hunt for photographs of relatives the next one, in which he and the professor were seated at a table, and right up beside them a newly-found relation—a lathe technician from the ultima Thule of Tula, or a vigneron from Verona—leaned into the frame. . .

Pascal was right: he'd scarcely informed the professor that he was coming to Italy, so he could take his government-paid vacation and have a rest from delivering smooth and brightly-colored flyers (which he would throw into a trashcan when there was nobody watching), when Ferrara invited him to come and visit. It's not enough that he met Pascal at the train station in Milan and, bald, nimble and cheerful in his deep crimson polo shirt and such unprofessorial sandals that Pascal was embarrassed, he handed him a bottle of mineral water and helped him carry his suitcase to the car, and then even took the stranger to his home, where there were booklets, in varying stages of dilapidation and display (one open to the first page, the next to the center spread), laid out all over the sofa and chairs. After taking a good, long, bewildered look, Pascal realized these were handwriting analysis manuals (a craft which in America, from what he'd observed, was only studied by charlatans), and Ferrara's wife, who was also nimble and whose hair had either been unevenly streaked by the sun or just poorly dyed in shades of pale yellow and rust, and who possessed the dryishness both in appearance and demeanor so typical to unattractive Milanese women, said that tomorrow she had a test.

"In Italy any personnel officer has the right to verify

the signature of a company employee. You can tell a lot from a signature," said Ferrara, explaining his wife's unusual interests, and Pascal felt at home again: here was a country, he thought, where you could live in an ancient house with a view of downtown and study the asexual reproduction of irrelevant worms, and not only not get into a rut, like what happens in the United States, when your whole life revolves around driving into and out of garages (out of your own, at home, where the door lifts up at the touch of a single button, and into a big, concrete one beneath an office building, store, or factory), but also be inspired by a practically extraneous tree planted by dead-men.

Pascal boasted that the roots of the tree dated back to the fifteenth century.

Just yesterday, having failed yet again to find a language in common with his mother (so much for the linguistics classes, he'd thought to himself), Pascal spent the whole day at a cemetery in Turin, crawling around the headstones and copying down their half-eroded epitaphs, moving from one stark granite vault to the next and seeing on each of them the repetition of names, passed down from century to century, from crypt to crypt—Laura, Claudina, Edoardo, Enrico (what use was it to the Claudina born in 1834 that a hundred years later a relation would also be called "Dina" and that she would die at precisely the same age of a gynecopathy—that wasn't clear to Pascal, and names that were similar annoyed him, like when he tried to determine who should get a letter: Williams Sol or his neighbor, Willy Solana), and here he was today with Ferrara, already discussing not only the dead, but also the living.

"Billy Grasso, *a strange old chap*," said Ferrara who, regardless of the fact that Pascal was a native Italian, attempted to speak English to him the whole time, after explaining that English had evolved into the language of studying worms, the language of scientific conferences, heated discussions and boring presentations, and that practicing it was essential.

Not yet having forgotten the desolate cemetery, where the only living person was the gravedigger, and even *his* face expressed deathly indifference as he walked past Pascal, dragging a broken, marble cross, which left a trail in the gravel behind him, Pascal rejoiced in this living, talking person (his joy was almost physical and he could feel it through the pores of his skin) and especially because Ferrara, regardless of his professorship and the worms, turned out to be just like him: inside them, despite their positions on unrelated branches of the family tree, there burned one and the same flame. This became apparent immediately after Ferrara handed Pascal a box of artifacts and photographs to acquaint himself with, which not only contained records of the "inhabitants'" birthdays, but which also housed their wedding albums, first teeth and, metaphorically speaking, their last dentures, and where there were also described the funny things they did, old folk-sayings, lameness. A collection of obituaries, snipped out of newspapers and paper-clipped together (at the very bottom), topped off the collection.

After the lunch Ferrara's wife had prepared of round flatbreads dusted with flour, mashed eggplant and hard pasta (a little harder than the mush you got in America), and also of tea, dressed up with excessively rich Sicilian sweets ("a student went to Sicily and brought them back—a smart lad, enchanted with worms!"), they discussed their unusual plan.

"It's a splendid opportunity to get acquainted with one of the specimens situated on the tree," the professor was saying to Pascal, and Pascal realized, judging by the energy with which Ferrara explained the situation, that the latter really was concerned about the fate of their distant relative who, in turn, happened to be related to the famous Italian book publishers, the Scarfati Brothers, and was connected to Pascal and Ferrara not so much by genes and epithelium as by anecdotes, handed down along a chain of generations and initially regarded as stories about family members, but then departing from their original source and becoming mere "slices of life."

"Billy Grasso is related to the well-to-do and famous Scarfatis, but regardless of this kinship he's as poor as a church mouse. He lives in one of the most impoverished and remote districts of Milan, in a social housing apartment, because he can't afford to pay."

Ferrara continued to narrate his story, and Pascal continued to be astonished.

"His mother was well-bred, knew foreign languages and how to dress, and either for this reason or another she'd never worked. She married a rich lawyer when she was young and bore him this very Billy, but then she got divorced.

Her ex-husband paid her several million lira a month, so she could continue to dress well and speak five languages, but then they nailed him for corruption and took everything away from him but the kitchen sink: his happiness, property, and bank deposits. And along with her wardrobe and son she had to move into a tiny hovel . . . "

Pascal listened attentively, without fully understanding why Ferrara knew so much about this Billy and why it had been so essential to wait for the arrival of one previously unknown relative, before he could call on another such relative, unrelated to the professor by blood.

"Let's not waste time talking," said Ferrara, and they took the velour-upholstered elevator downstairs, got into the professorial green Toyota Prius, buckled their seatbelts, and Pascal began to watch the classy high-rise buildings become fewer and transform into smaller, middle-sized dwellings for the middle class, and then grow larger again and become some kind of uncolored, and crudely unfinished prefab housing for those who had been squeezed out to the peripheries by a poverty-stricken, merciless life.

"He's an interesting specimen—he quotes Sophocles and Petronius, knows Latin perfectly, keeps up with developments in literature, music, the theater. . . I saw him about ten years ago, at the funeral of his mother's sister, only that once."

"What does he do for a living?" asked Pascal with interest.

"At one time Billy considered himself a brilliant photographer, though like his mother, he never worked anywhere. . . He's much worse off now, and of course the stomach cancer doesn't help. I'm afraid it won't be long before he dies."

The professorial Prius came to a stop by a dreary prefab building. Having covered his guest's suitcase in the trunk with either a stained old sketch-board, or a coat that was just as old, and covered in sloppy and slovenly stains, the professor learnedly remarked: "This is a bad part of town, you've got to keep your eyes and ears open around here," and, unhurriedly but dexterously maneuvering his feet, clad in a pair of leather sandals without socks, he walked up to the entrance.

"It's Billy!" exclaimed Pascal suddenly.

There was an old man walking along the street in a ragged cashmere sweater, with the moiré collar of a once fashionable shirt sticking out at the neck. His trousers had been painstakingly pressed, but the fabric was inferior; he was wearing a trendy cap on his head, but it was made of cheap polyester.

"Hurry, or he'll get away—after him!" said Pascal, tugging at Ferrara.

"It's not him, but there's a resemblance," uttered Ferrara, after quickening his step and turning his head excitedly in the direction of the cashmere old man. This bit of theater had enchanted him, and he seemed even more energetic, his crimson polo crimsoned, and his bald scalp glistened.

"News about Billy reaches me roughly once a year, at Christmas, when one of my relatives pays us her annual visit, and it tends to worsen progressively. First I found out they'd been left penniless, then last year his aged mother, with whom he'd lived here, died (she was the only one who'd ever encouraged his pursuit of photography), and they say that following her death Billy began to behave very strangely, so I wouldn't be surprised if he didn't even let us in the door!"

With these words the professor pressed button thirty-four. Someone with a hoarse voice from behind the panel of iron mesh over the intercom started clearing his throat.

"What? What did he say?" asked Pascal, who'd missed a few of the jerky remarks that Ferrara had exchanged with the wilted, decrepit voice crawling out through the iron grating, but the professor was already dragging Pascal behind him, with the words: "We're in luck, he's home and would be happy to see us!"

The elevator smelled of urine; it was suspiciously

damp on the floor in front. Ferrara looked at the shiny wet area attentively, and just as attentively lifting his sandaled, sockless feet up high, he walked around it.

The door to Billy's apartment was ajar. Pascal knew from his experience as a mailman that the doors to poor apartments were always set ajar. Sometimes, when he walked into an apartment like that with a delivery, the recipients didn't realize it was from their free, legal-aid lawyer or former workplace (which they'd had to leave due to illness), and backed away from him at once: "No-no, we're not paying for that!," they'd say, thinking he was trying to sell them something, and Pascal would patiently explain that there was no money required, that he was the mailman, and here somebody had sent them a present. The suspicion in the eyes of the recipients would disappear agonizingly slowly, and when Pascal recounted these stories to his colleagues at the post office they looked at him in such disbelief that Pascal realized he was arguably the most considerate and sensitive mailman of them all . . .

Evidently Billy had heard their voices, because through the partially open door they heard: "Come in, come in!," and when Pascal walked up to the doorstep (the apartment was thick with the odor of an elderly person and his solitude), there to meet him, shuffling and hawking, was a disheveled old man with bad, blotchy skin (Pascal instantly noticed the wisps of hair on his head and the unshaven tufts on his cheeks), in a thick cotton sweatshirt bearing the name of a British university with no relationship to him whatsoever, and bare feet. Pascal tried to pretend he didn't notice these black, swollen feet covered with cracked skin and sores, but his eyes kept gravitating toward them involuntarily. "Looks like gout," whispered Ferrara, who also noticed everything.

Billy started coughing, and when he was through coughing he asked for a cigarette. His visage was bloated, but full face you could still discern the young man in him, lean in his youth (this was clear to Pascal at once from a photo in the living-room which, as it turned out afterwards, proved to be a portrait of Billy's little-boyish daughter, both of which—the daughter and the portrait—he took pride in). "She's a theater actress and playwright," he elucidated.

The skin hung loosely from his neck, and his large aquiline nose added to his puffy face a certain rapaciousness, which was incongruous with his unhealthy doughiness, and his whole neglected appearance clashed with that of the red-cheeked mailman and the well-groomed, elderly professor concerned about his cholesterol.

Pascal got a half-crumpled pack of cigarettes out of the breast pocket of his wrinkled white shirt (he hesitated to wear black in Italy) and fished out two—all that were left. "Thank you!" croaked Billy with dignity, and Pascal thought, now there was a coincidence for you, to just run out of smokes and right then and there have a couple of uninvited guests show up with some tobacco, but then he noticed a dirty dish on a bookshelf; there were disgusting ash stains on it, as well as some unsmoked, virginally untouched cigarettes, and he felt awkward, as if he'd caught Billy in a lie.

"We're all family here," pronounced Professor Ferrara with a smile, and he looked affectionately at the coughing and wheezing Billy. "Here I'm a professor, and he's a mailman."

"The professor studies worms," added Pascal, so as to say something, at least, and portray them both favorably. The professor stiffened. But after all, once Billy found out the professor studied worms he'd realize straight away that they'd come here from the desire to get acquainted and not, for example, to haggle over the books put out by the Scarfati Brothers Publishing House. . .

The books in question really were on the shelves in closely packed rows.

"Why, your aunt was a well-known authoress, wasn't she?" asked Ferrara. "I was at her funeral."

"Yes, you're absolutely right," nodded Billy, and he lit a cigarette. He was smoking, and the smoke streamed unhurriedly upwards; Billy's eyes were watering and he started coughing again.

Beyond the door, which Billy had gone ahead and left ajar, they could hear shuffling, and then angry voices. "I'll look into it!" said Ferrara, and he exited. A minute later he was back: "Your neighbors have come home, Billy. They're cursing about us smashing up their car . . ."

"They're lunatics, don't pay any attention to them," replied Billy, inhaling. "The whole building's like that."

A cry rang out on the other side of the door.

"Billy, should we perhaps close the door?" suggested Ferrara affably. He was gracious and delicate, as though he were afraid to disturb the established order of things.

"Oh, don't worry, they won't come in here," replied Billy. "I don't know how many times they've already complained about that car, but their car was stolen in 2005."

Ferrara added: "And I was surprised as well. Our car is parked directly across from the entrance, whereas they claim theirs was smashed around the corner."

"Just wait, they'll be back in an hour claiming something else."

Something heavy banged against the door.

"It's like this every day here," said Billy; his cigarette had gone out, and he started groping around on the table in search of a lighter.

The professor, having excused himself, left to go to the toilet for a second and returned from there looking worried and anxious: "Billy, I noticed the water in the bidet is running; you forgot to turn off the faucet."

Billy puffed at his cigarette butt and, when he got right down to the filter, he placed it in a second dirty metal saucer that was sitting on the table. He was extremely polite and quiet, and he agreed with everything: it was the way a subordinate behaved in the presence of the boss, from whom he didn't know what to expect.

"The water's always running in there; the plumber came and said it couldn't be fixed anymore."

"I get it now," remarked Ferrara. "Here I thought you didn't know about it."

"Didn't you ask about my auntie?" asked Billy. He got up from the table in the sweatshirt that hadn't been laundered in a long time, and started rooting around in a chest, where some books had been dumped. "These are her manuscript compositions, and here are the volumes bound in leather by the Scarfati Brothers; I won't charge much."

Professor Ferrara looked at Pascal steadily and meaningfully and announced: "Billy, he's got to get back to Turin, so we've only dropped in for a very short while. We're going straight to the train station from here."

Billy was peering into the bookshelf, as if his eyes were endowed with the sense of touch and were supposed to make direct physical contact with the letters (Pascal noticed that Billy's eyelashes were long and silky, and that they were brushing against the book-bindings, dilapidated by time), and then he pulled out a small volume with whitish veins on the spine. "Like little worms," thought Pascal.

"Here it is! Only twenty euros—is it a deal?"

"No, we don't need any books," replied Ferrara, declining the offer.

"Letters!" exclaimed the old man with a start. "I've got her letters; after all, she carried on a correspondence with many of the writers of the day, and the Futurist Marinetti was her confidant."

He added a few words in Latin, but Pascal didn't understand their relevance.

Right behind Ferrara they walked into the entrance hall.

Billy went back into the room and returned from there with a canvas bag of the supermarket type packed full of something:

"Here, just before you arrived I was sorting through her letters; they're genuine—nobody's read them but me!"

"No, we don't need them," said Ferrara. "Thank you anyway," and he glanced at Billy's cracked, swollen feet compassionately.

The latter continued talking: "Just yesterday I was re-reading the entries in her diary, and she describes her meeting with Montale! Oohs and ahs, but then there follows a detailed analysis of his poems . . . My aunt was anything but stupid."

Ferrara inquired: "Billy, are you feeling alright?"

Billy looked awful. He had big bags under his eyes and a piece of fabric around his wrist, and the fly on his bagged out pants was half open (Pascal thought that maybe he'd started to do it up, but then forgot, without zipping it all the way).

"A nurse came by today to give me an injection," said Billy, shaking his hand, and then he added: "Enzo Montale, the Nobel Laureate."

Pascal looked at him in confusion.

"No, Eugenio Monti," muttered Billy, adding something else, but again Pascal couldn't decipher his words.

"Monti, Monti . . . ," Billy continued to repeat and, having bitten down on his lip, he roamed through the labyrinths of his failing memory. Finally he got it straight:

"Eugenio Monti—they were talking about his victories on the bobsled on the television today, whereas Aunt Mimma, of course, was acquainted with Montale."

"Why, you've got a full-length portrait of her hanging right here! She was a very classy woman—you see, Pascal? She was friends with my grandmother; they used to call on each other up at their villas in the summer, and in the winter they would exchange recipes," exclaimed Ferrara.

It was dark in the corridor; one of the bulbs had burned out, so the old portrait, rendered in oil—of a pretty, elegant woman in a fitted dress and high, lace-up boots—on the shabby, peeling wall was difficult to make out. What's more, a layer of dust and many years had done its part, and it looked like the portrait had blackened.

"There's his aunt!" repeated Professor Ferrara with a distinct knowledgeability in his voice, as though he were showing that he'd studied the family tree closely and knew everything now.

Pascal lifted his head and stared hard at the portrait.

"It's Mamma," said Billy quietly.

"No, it's not your Mamma; it's a famous portrait and it was painted by a well-known artist. Your aunt even became this portrait-artist's mistress when she was still young, in nineteen hundred and thirty-one," said Ferrara. "See for yourself, her name's written right here—Mimma!"

"It's Mamma, and I wrote those letters myself. What's written is Mamma. So it isn't Mimma at all," objected Billy. His eyebrows were raised, and it seemed like he was surprised himself that they'd suddenly gotten into this argument.

The word "Mamma" sounded unexpectedly tender from Billy's lips, having previously spoken so hoarsely, and Pascal thought it had to be anything but simple: to live your whole life, up to the age of seventy-four, in the same apartment as your mother, to depend on her completely and be her permanent companion, and then to lose her.

"No-no, I saw this portrait on the Internet, and it said this was the authoress Mimma," said Ferrara with certainty, and Pascal noticed that Billy was having second thoughts. Uncertainty flashed in his watery eyes. He stood unsteadily on his black feet, his hands trembling.

Billy stood there at a loss, and Pascal could see the course of his thoughts on his face; his lips stirred slightly, and his forehead strained, as though he were trying to find some way to vindicate his assertions, but he just couldn't find anything that would confute his visitors outright. Since he could find no refutation, it seemed the pendulum of his thoughts had begun to swing toward the assertions of his guest, and toward the idea that the portrait did indeed portray Aunt Mimma, and not his mother at all.

They left: the bald Professor Ferrara in his sandals and impeccably ironed crimson polo shirt and the rumpled, awkwardly red-cheeked Pascal, dripping with sweat in his white, overly flimsy, almost see-through shirt; Pascal-the-mailman, who would long suffer torments now, in the belief that casually and offhand he'd planted doubt in the soul of a man preparing to die . . . , and who was agonizing over the fact that he and the professor had descended upon poor Billy's apartment, in order to fill in the details of their tree, and almost taken away everything Billy had left; Billy, the most downtrodden and insignificant relative on their family tree, the relative whose beloved mother they'd taken away with their words, and in whom they had unwittingly reinforced the forgetfulness of a man already lapsing into dementia, by completely painting over and mutilating the portrait of her, so painfully familiar to her son—transiently, as casual, curious enquirers, who liked to be in on things, be they worms or people.

(trans. Krystyna A. Steiger)

Ai Weiwei's Owls

A rectangular banner hung on the circular exhibition hall. Frida walked up to it and had a look. The words "You Are Here," printed on it in decisive orange pencil, gave her hope. Not Frida, of course, but Rita. By not articulating her /r/'s the American way, she threw off—and simultaneously scared off—anyone wanting to get acquainted. To the question "Arita?," she replied "yes," all the more quickly to disengage. And even when they affirmed, "so it's Frida?," she nodded. She acquiesced to any name.

Bending miopically and scoliotically, she read "Playground 4: Natural Materials, Fun Children's Activities." Then, first letter of her name alternating, she walked for a long time, past crumbling structures permanently under repair, past houses of indeterminate colors, where the spots in need of touching up were indicated with light-blue ovals, past tractors that were out of date, and even out of place on a Sunday, past locked-up portable toilets, past a pale gray, four-story building, with the fire stairs torn away at the third. A victim of spatial cretinism, she turned her attention to a sign on the door: "Park Police." A marker to turn back. Almost right by the road. Plot 31. But easy to access for seniors.

The sun beat down. Her daughter and son shuffled along behind: the unsociable Frida wanted them to learn to play with other children.

There were cones and brushwood piled up in the clearing, under the number four. Girls were weaving things out of sedge grass. Boys were holding up an unsteady table, fashioned out of a stump and trimmed aspen branches. Frida's little daughter and son didn't know what to amuse themselves with; they stood over beside their unfamiliar peers. The latter were digging in the sand. When they'd finished, they took out their lunch. Sandwiches with bits of earth; a white bun pressed into a black hole with the heel of a shoe. There was a man with a bare pate talking about himself close by. "I'm a cavalry-man," he explained to some women, who were rubbing lotion into their reddening shoulders.

A little boy in a stained and soggy t-shirt, who'd plopped down beside his mother, sat drinking out of a flask she'd handed him. The rest were climbing posts and rocks, like ants. "My head hurts." The mother replied: "But you're so proud of yourself—look how much you've built in all." Her son repeated: "But my head hurts so much." Again the mother said: "You've accomplished so much today! And now sit in the shade for a while and rest."

The boys had finally steadied the table. No sooner had they turned their attention from their woodworking to the rocks, than it fell over again. The girls had improvised a hut and all squeezed into it, knocking the fir branches off the 'roof.'

In keeping with the adults' plan, the children were learning to commune with nature.

Nobody had looked up.

After adjusting the bucket hat on her son's head, Frida saw a couple of pensioners holding a map. They walked straight up to the playground. Myopically and sclerotically studying their guidebook, the old folks were trying to figure something out. After a short discussion, they looked up, laughed, and continued on their way.

Another pair walked up. These pensioners were wearing bucket hats, like the children.

Arita-Frida raised her head.

Up in the tall oak tree, beneath which the man was telling the women about the lives of horses and soldiers, there hung some casks. They were reminiscent of ceramic circuit breakers, clay goggle-eyes of enormous proportions, gigantic floaters.

By the time Frida-Arita's eyes had made their way to the ninth, and last, bluish-white cask, she was dizzy. This was where a decisive orange pencil would come in handy. To stick into the ground and lean back against, as if it were a staff. There were people who wouldn't think twice about drawing arrows directing others.

At the entrance to the park she too had taken a guidebook on the unusual, open-air exhibition, although she was afraid that because of the children's project she wouldn't make it there. She grabbed it and immediately noticed a star beside the number four, meaning that this very clearing, where the children were getting acquainted with shaggy, gnarly and knotted nature, was the location of a work of art.

It was entitled "Hollows for Owls."

Frida recalled an interview she'd recently read.

The fifty-five-year-old sculptor Ai Weiwei said he'd never wanted children, he simply lived his life sculpting various objects, but when his assistant unexpectedly became pregnant by him, he was reassuring: "Well of course have it." He said: "Owls are a unique symbol in China. They sleep with one eye slightly open and everybody's afraid of them, whereas I've held them in awe since childhood . . . So I made these hollows for them, replicas of vessels typical to the Ming Dynasty. May they fly in!"

Frida eyed the flaxen-haired children seated on the tree stump. She looked up at the casks. In the midst of the living foliage this ancient Chinese pretension looked as alien as a bare-metal stent in a coronary artery. Weiwei had made an opening in the bottom of each of them. The owls would definitely be cozy inside, but they were nowhere in sight. Hollows for owls that weren't there.

Arita thought: "How is it that nobody gives a damn, that nobody in the clearing has raised their head and seen this remarkable creation by 'the Chinese Warhol'—an unconventional, contemporary master. . ." The sun beat down. The casks hung on the branches. The owls hid away from human eyes . . . A few miles from there, in a town called Colma, wrapped in a white shroud, laid to rest deep down beneath the concrete and the reddish-black soil, with a shock of red hair and hundreds of unrealized dreams, lay Rita-Frida's father, like a bright installation in a gloomy museum, like a combination of earth and plastic in a coffin padded with dusty-violet felt.

(Trans. Krystyna A. Steiger)

Four Hands

<u>Mother</u>: A short, black-haired jackdaw, she cordially opens mouth, door, piano. She walks right in, sits, begins playing right off. Bravo, Nonna, says her husband. It really is bravura. On the walls: candelabras and handicrafts created from nature's cornucopia. She can buy anything she wants, but isn't above her own handiwork. Gay elation: "Know what I'm playing?", then acute condemnation: "Surely you're joking, not the boyish Shainsky! It's Chopin!"

The parting gift's a shell, an abalone. She's drawn to the cradle the guests brought, and the snuffling, still-nameless creature. "I keep telling mine to try, but they're in no hurry to make a grandma out of me. I'd nanny her day in and day out! Keep trying!" An ostensibly joking nod to her weak son—some software specialist—and his strong, muscular wife.

<u>Father</u>: Used to a first-class pianist too, but ruined his reach (fishing), his back (sciatica), and the joy of music (drinking). For days on end he fiddles with his boat, named in honor of his black-haired helpmeet. Not too tall, not too bright. Looks like a bowlegged Cossack. There's pictures all over the house of him and his catfish: he's happy and bewhiskered, the catfish has whiskers too, but is dead. Father lives, but without will, like the forte pedal under his wife's foot. He hems and haws in parting; he's spackling, fudging it, fixing his

oarlocks as he sits on the hull.

<u>Son</u>: A soloist as a kid, went on stage with the orchestra (coughing in the auditorium, parents stock-still), then abandoned the bow to bond with the Italian people. On the way through Italy to the United States he washed cars, hawked pins and mangy matreshka dolls on the sidewalk, and now he's afraid of everything: of being alone, of being single (there was always so much mother that now the emptiness must be filled with a life companion), of his mother's fury, his father's indifference.

<u>Son's Wife</u>: They had the wedding on a boat, but not on the "Nonnushka," on another one, big and beaming, that all the white trash could fit on. Fraternization of intellectual Soviet Jews with the wife's brother and cousin: an arrogant American soldier-boy who went AWOL twice, and a slutty secretary. The young wife had three pairs of parents, all rednecks: her father—knobby head, shit-kicker boots—got serially divorced, each new woman turning into wife-stepmother-mother.

Five years after the wedding: a rented apartment, shelter dogs (biters, who after a few training sessions at fifty bucks a pop had to be put down), snow and skis in Sierra Nevada, rest and sun in Israel, trips to India, Japan, Katmandu. Finally: their own home, with a leaky faucet that won't stop dripping. Son gives mother the full report: yes, I bought a house, no, I haven't fixed the pipes yet.

<u>Mother</u> anxiously awaits a grandchild. The first few

tries are failures, but the fourth time, finally, the belly appears and swells serenely. In the sixth month the

Wife announced that she's a lesbian

Mother says that she refuses to have anything to do with a daughter-in-law like this, and

Father, with his catatonic, photogenic catfish, can't come up with anything to say or do except repeat after the mother and continue floating on the boat named after her

Son is in total shock. What is to be done? Got to fix the faucet and sell the house, now. Got to find another wife, and fast (after all, he can't make it alone, but he'd had all kinds of girls in bed before the wedding: students with improbable majors, spiteful ice queens, pimply nothing-muches with their salicylic acid)

Wife: Wanted to get married to be like everybody else, "to have a real wedding too, with guests, with nice stuff," and so tried to smother all feeling for the female sex, but she couldn't do a thing about it

Son is in shock

Mother and Father are in total denial: she's not any daughter-in-law of ours, her daughter is no grandchild to us, and you, if you keep acting like this and visiting her, you won't be any son to us

Son about his not-yet-born daughter: this isn't the life I wanted for myself, for her

Wife: I wasn't even looking for anything, after all Sonya was already here under my heart, but then I saw Her (we went to the same school as kids) and knew right away

<u>Son</u>: My ex-wife and I got together for coffee, and I was suddenly struck: how did I get along with her for so many years, this completely foreign person? This made me feel a little better, and right then Sonya started knocking… just as though she were waiting for me to fly in from Colorado (because now we live in different states).

Nothing happened that day, but the next morning I got a call at the hotel and I came right away, and there's my ex-wife in labor, in the bathtub so everything's natural, no anesthetics, as nature wills… I was holding her by one hand, and her live-in lover by the other. Then my Sonya came into the world, with her tiny little nose and nails… striking how much she looks like me…

<u>Mother</u> and <u>Father</u>: she doesn't exist for us. We don't have any granddaughter. We don't have any former daughter-in-law. There's no such people.

They go to the piano and play a piece for four hands.

(Trans. Anne Fisher)

The Autograph

"Would you like to hear John Cale in concert?" Vladimir asked. Intense and in tune with everything ahead of its time, he had a soul patch with a tint of grey hair, just like his idol, except Cale's was dyed hot pink.

Her only connection to "Velvet Underground" was her first husband. Much older than her, he was a concert promoter in New York who once made Warhol a proposition. During the business lunch in a bistro, Andy was silent, "not even mumbling. And later, through his manager, he declined anyway."

Her first husband died of cancer three years ago.

Her second husband begged her to listen to one of Cale's songs and, appreciating its edginess and Vladimir's eagerness to spend the evening with her, she nodded "yes" (she often was too immersed in dark thoughts to be able to tolerate daylight) and then "yes" once again, to obtain his autograph after the concert was over.

As the robust Cale in a jean jacket and boots left the old-style ballroom's stage (velvet curtains and gold on the ceiling), they exited through the back door onto the street. With a dumpster on the left and a dilapidated hotel in front, the barely lit street was lifeless except for three people. A determined lad in a pea coat holding a rolled poster, a gentleman with a ponytail, and a wiry man with a guitar, squatting and smoking a joint.

A concert tour bus was parked outside and its driver stood up, scratched himself and pulled down a t-shirt over a jellied belly. A beat-up sedan crawled by and then stopped. Two rough-looking young punks got out, luminescent stripes on their pants and shoes flashing, with sheets of paper in hand.

"Who is it today?" one of the punks asked. "John who? From a band formed by Warhol? Oh yeah, we want him!"

"Professional autograph hunters," Vladimir whispered. "They have no idea… But the guy with the ponytail is holding the famous 'banana' record designed by Warhol. If the banana's unpeeled, it's worth a thousand bucks."

Suddenly she overheard what the wiry, wheat-mustachioed man in a hat, resembling an exhausted and slightly effeminate cowboy, said to the punks:

"When I go to festivals with my son, I tell him: everybody closer to your age is yours and everybody closer to my age is mine. Do you folks like women or men?"

"Women." She heard an assertive voice and felt threatened. Brandishing sexual prowess outside a concert venue. Unsettled, she looked around: she was the only woman here, at 1 in the morning, waiting for an autograph from a famous man.

At the dumpster, a homeless person in fuzzy orange gloves that looked like furry paws raised himself over the edge and peered inside. Down the street prostitutes in tights exited one car and approached another. A peculiar hunched figure was walking toward them carrying something huge and misshapen on its back. Coming close, the figure stopped, lowered what turned out to be a mattress, positioned it on the ground and sat on it, listening to headphones around his neck.

The ponytailed man stared in front of himself, his mouth tense. She had seen him in the audience earlier with a "First Aid" badge and some medical instruments: refined and aloof, in thin glasses, he reminded her of Chekhov, Vladimir's favorite writer, who doubled as a doctor and treated the underserved.

She thought an autograph from a member of "Velvet Underground" would connect her to her first husband who'd once attempted to rent a venue to Warhol's band. She still missed him, at times experiencing a severe depression which severed her from the rest of the world, but was afraid to tell Vladimir she wanted to visit her late husband's grave.

Vladimir elbowed her: "The Ponytail accidentally peeled his banana," he said. "Now the record's lost half of its value."

Vladimir explained: "The young guy was inching toward the door and shoved aside the Ponytail, who nearly dropped the record on the dirty sidewalk. He tried to catch it and grabbed it instinctively by the banana's stem—which separated. He looks so desperate now. This is so sad!"

And she thought: "Sad, indeed, this night and this narrow street… And these people huddling on a filthy mattress… scrounging dumpsters for food… following artists they don't care about… Searching for sex at music festivals… All this, coupled with the ghosts of my past… All immensely attuned, as though prewritten, yet longingly sad."

Multiple Children

1

The Saint Card

This is what happened minutes ago to me as in a dream, in the city of Oakville. At lunchtime I punched out at my online ordering company and trod my usual way to a grocery store. Passing by a gas station, where a sun-glassed cop used to hide hunting for speeders but today wasn't present, I decided to call, on a whim, the nanny for my four-year-old daughter. In an energetic, assertive conversation with her I emphasized that occasionally cars jump the curb onto the sidewalk and run over the pedestrians, and that she must look both ways when exiting the front door with little Liz.

After I hung up, satisfied that the nanny was empathetic toward my multiple motherly warnings, I decided to swing by Beauty Supply and buy a discounted scrub with Dead Sea salts for my skin. With a plastic bag swinging in my right hand, giving me a feeling of freedom, I entered a New Age grocery store and tasted a sample, noticing that the regular cook with gray bohemian hair wasn't on duty and couldn't ask why he sees me so often and never with any produce.

Having tried a gentrified enchilada, I walked

outside: it was the end of the week, and, inundated by rushing customers and finger-numbing repetitive work, I was looking forward to the weekend. When passing through a gas station, next to a car undergoing a gastrological operation with a pipe stuck in its stomach, I saw a miniature picture. It lay on the ground between two oil spots.

Waiting till a pickup truck next to the laminated bright picture drove away, with its tanned tank-topped inhabitants with gold crosses, I picked it up and put it into my pocket, afraid that its anonymous owner was going to claim my serendipitous find. A gas station attendant gave me a look. After checking that he was now distracted by a customer, I put the picture close to my eyes and read, "Santo Toribio Romo, Ruega por Nosotros, a martyr." Afraid to encounter the rightful owner, some Mexican immigrant, whom the Saint Toribio Romo protected at the border and in the desert, I hid it in my pocket again.

Then I saw a dark car swerving toward me while making a turn.

Every day I walked this very sidewalk and saw approaching cars, yet something was strange about this one, since instead of turning, it continued going straight.

Everything happened so fast that I had no time to get scared or process information. The dark-blue car jumped the curb and ended up only a couple of inches away from me on the sidewalk. Later I realized that if

I hadn't stopped at the gas station and fumbled with the laminated martyr, I would have reached this place a few moments earlier and would have been hit by this car.

If I hadn't bent down to lift Toribio Romo from earth, I would have been dead.

A Volkswagen "bug" stood on the pedestrian path.

I noticed that it was brand new. The long-haired young woman inside was visibly shaken, and when I tried to go around the "bug," I heard her repeating, "I lost control, I lost control; I was driving and steering and then I don't know what happened." Touching the smooth laminate of the martyr, I was going back to work, but because of the stunned faces around me (a crowd was gathering) I understood that the car on the sidewalk was not your typical thing.

A man asked if I was okay, but I didn't answer, afraid that because of my accent he would have to ask me the same question again. I heard a hissing sound and saw that it was air coming out of the "bug's right front wheel. It was bent and missing a hubcap.

Tracing its fate and locating it two yards away lying lifeless, I realized that this was the exact place from which I had called the *nyanya* a half an hour earlier, when I was still on my way to the grocery store. It was the exact spot where, as though in a premonition, I mentioned cars jumping onto the sidewalk in my phone conversation with her,—and here I was, and the sidewalk, and the car which had indeed jumped.

Two Indian-looking males from the nearby bank (red badges were attached to their shirts) were encouraging the driver to go in reverse and leave the sidewalk. The longhaired driver replied that she couldn't move because she was in shock and had lost control of the car. The men insisted, but the woman was frozen, afraid to raise her hands to the wheel.

I picked up the hubcap and noticed that my right hand had become dirty; now I had to wash the dirt off prior to touching the martyr. I placed the hubcap right next to the "bug" and went back toward the building where I worked. From afar, I noticed that the driver had exited the car and was walking toward the hubcap in her high heels. I came back to my cubicle and googled the name of Santo Toribio Romo.

He was an attractive young man with dreamy eyes who was killed in the first part of the 20th century during a Mexican war. As a priest, he lived in a small parish and was still in bed when thugs burst into his room and aimed their guns at his heart.

I'd learned that Toribio Romo was killed because of his faith and after canonization became a patron of immigrants.

2

TO THE MOON

A hasty Monday morning with hectic movements up and down the stairs in this three-bedroom, three-storey condo, the gathering of a maroon wallet, a gift from my Italian mother-in-law, a cell phone, a magnetic key from my work, and a comb. The keys for my car and home are missing: just yesterday my four-year old daughter shook them triumphantly in front of me and my husband, and we removed them from her and placed them on a table. Today they are gone.

It's 7:10 a.m. and if I don't leave within a few minutes, I'll be late for my phone shift at an online ordering company. I try to remember: after we took the keys from Liz, what happened next? She made us sit on a couch, tied two belts together and placed them over our knees, announcing that we were going to the Moon.

Together with us was Tatiana, a huge striped plush toy with steely blue eyes named in honor of a Siberian tiger that had attacked an annoying zoo visitor. All four of us fit on the small couch, and after the cosmic ship reached the Moon, Liz, in a firefighter's hard hat, proclaimed that we had to drag out Tatiana. We promptly did, pulling her by the paws. Liz was very excited, since Tatiana was able to see the beautiful Moon. After a short stop, we pulled her out of space and seated her back on the couch to rest after an excruciating assignment; none of this, however, involved handling my keys.

It was 7:16 a.m. and, anticipating traffic, I was afraid I would not make it today for my phone shift. Right at this moment the phone rang; it was a frantic long-distance call from my mother-in-law. Reluctant to wake up my husband exhausted by the daily activities of his flower shop, I spoke to her mixing up English and Italian words, trying to add compassion to both. My father-in-law was quite sick. Not only did he barely remember that he had a son in America, but he had forgotten the names of his brothers (he had six of them, all living in the Calabria region) and was oblivious of his own age.

"Today he flew to the Moon," said my mother-in-law. "This is all he remembers... our cleaning lady's name is Vittoria, and today he told me that he was going to take Vittoria with him to the Moon. You know, in the sixties, when your Soviet sputnik flew there, your father-in-law went to several kiosks and bought up a hundred newspapers with the announcement, because he thought of it as a groundbreaking event. Now he is flying himself."

There was something eerie, I thought, in this overlapping of my daughter's Moon to which we all flew and her grandfather's Moon where he went with the cleaning lady Vittoria, but it was 7:25 a.m. and I was late. My husband woke up and approached me, realizing that I was talking to his mother in Italy; he attempted to grab the receiver but I had already hung up. I queried him about where my keys were, but he got so upset about his father's condition that he started shouting, telling me that I should not blame him for constantly losing my things. He said that today there was a big funeral, that he had to prepare a large order for it with a spray and a cross, and that he was in a hurry himself and not able to find my damn keys.

Saying this, several times he repeated the name of the deceased, each time changing a vowel, "Shavella, Shevella, Shovella," and I asked him to show respect for the dead. In response to this he shouted that he had the fucking funeral to make flowers for, and I was distracting him with this search for my damn keys. He added that if I woke up our daughter, she would start jumping around preventing him from making a perfect funeral wreath.

The time was 7:36 a.m., and I envisioned my supervisor clocking me and assigning others to ask, "Which product from the catalog are you interested in?" But at least I could make it to the following hourly phone shift.

I raced up to the third floor and touched my daughter's shoulder, "Wake up!" She slept soundly, with a blanket falling over the side of the bed. Once she awoke, she rubbed her eyes and said that she had played "hide-and-seek" with my keys and they were in the garage. When together we walked to the garage filled with dry flowers, baskets, bears, and funeral wreaths, she said that, unnerved by our argument, she had gotten confused. Then she whispered that instead of the garage she actually meant the laundry room. It was 7:40 a.m..

We went to the second floor, my husband mad and late for the funeral, me mad and late for my shift, our daughter composed and calm. She led us to a blue bucket beneath the lowest shelf in the laundry room, and after retrieving my keys, I sent her back to her bed. While I was racing after her to the third floor to make sure she went under the blanket, my husband shouted that he was awfully late for "Shavella, Shevella, Shovella," and I shouted back to him that he had no regard for the deceased.

Later he called me at work to apologize and reported that the funeral had been postponed.

"For how long?" surprised, exclaimed I, and he answered, "For an indefinite time."

"It's so sweet! Your daughter hid your keys to keep you from going to work. She wanted to spend more time with you, to postpone this separation," commented my boss, smiling.

And I thought that the parents wanted to spend more time with the 41-year old Shavella Jerome: keep her with them for a little longer, even though they couldn't talk; hold her hand silently; kiss her cold forehead; cry over her life that ended so early in a drunken fight with her boyfriend; postpone her trip to a faraway Moon.

3

Camera in the Shower

He is barely two years old; his mother is twenty-seven, in jail.

In a daycare in the Mission District in San Francisco, Willy eats meatballs which his nanny calls *ezhiki*—little hedgehogs in Russian. He is dark-skinned and very composed; his diaper shows from under his bulging pants, his amber necklace—from under his freshly laundered checkered shirt. He already walks steadily and is drawn mostly to men, not having seen his mother for months and being apprehensive of women.

His mother eats plain white beans for breakfast, a white bean burrito for dinner, a white bean mish-mash for supper before going to sleep in her cell. The connection between her and Willy is only sporadic. From the detention center, she can call only collect and her mobile phone operator blocks collect calls. When she reaches her son, the signal is weak.

Willy's father comes to the daycare and mentions that Willy's mom, an Italian medical student, is being detained in Southern California. Every time she flew from Rome to Frisco, she was sent back, for lack of legal status in the U.S. This time she missed Willy so much that she crossed the border illegally and was caught. The guards didn't even look at the toddler's snapshots she kept in her purse.

Willy eats very accurately, his nanny reports, and he is making progress. He knows how to hold a fork and a spoon. After finishing *ezhiki*, the two-year old washes his hands with liquid hand soap. His father, who works as a chef in an Italian restaurant and at night designs websites for social change, to pay for childcare, complains to the nanny that in the detention center the guards are rude to inmates. "And there are no video cameras in the male showers!" he exclaims with a surprise, "only in the women's." "This is disgusting," he adds.

Willy's nanny reports that today Willy was especially good on the playground. When she asked him to pick up his toys, he obliged right away and went to a sandbox. There, he saw that a little girl had apprehended his yellow spade. She came to the playground with her mother, who used to bring a guitar and sing "You are my sunshine" to all the kids willing to listen. Willie not only waited for the girl to finish her playing, but he placed his toys in a bag and carried them all the way home and up the stairs, without complaint.

Willy starts wailing at night.

4

Across the Stage

* * *

During the other performances, she could not sit still in her chair and would walk back and forth between the fifth and the tenth rows, sometimes disappearing from view when crouching on the floor and apparently plucking the wooden planks or pulling the carpet. Or she would walk up to a young girl distracted by a cookie her mother was offering, and she would move the girl's head toward the stage with the words, "Watch! You have to watch! Don't eat!" If somebody tried to approach her, she would run away hissing and shouting like a disturbed little puppy, and the actors on the stage would shake nervously but would continue their play.

The names of the plays were "Peter and the Wolf" and "Little Red Riding Hood," and, attending them, she was smartly dressed in color-coordinated outfits with pink embroidery on the pocket of a crocheted jacket that matched the ornaments on her white fitted pants. Her eyes were of a deep brown color, but when she would stare at you, you would see that they had a strange grayish shade. Aside from her wild behavior in the theatre, she was a sweet girl of three and half years.

We, the parents, for whom she was the "late child"

(it took a long time for her to arrive and a prolonged preparation of both the potential mother and father, including psychological counseling, genetic testing, and therapeutic walks in the forest), prepared her well for the next performance of "Peter Pan."

Shamed by other parents that our only offspring was walking around during the play disturbing the actors, we purchased a book and a CD, and took turns with little "Miss L" (that's how she asked us to call her), explaining to her what was going on and how interesting this particular piece of literature was. Should we note that coming to the U.S. from two different European countries and meeting in the Silicon Valley, we had never heard about this play. Moreover, while reading it to our daughter, we never understood what it meant. We only tried to interest her in the action so that she could develop at a speed appropriate to her age.

It was we who again reminded her to be extra attentive and listen to every word said on the stage. We approached the theater building, walking across the parking lot with our "Miss L", her legs bent and suspended in the air between her European parents. I held her left hand and her father, her right.

Dragging "Miss L" to the theatre, we reminded her that she should follow this play about the orphans who didn't want to grow old, and that we would be so proud of her if she sat still throughout performance.

Were we to be given another chance to relive this moment, we probably would have thought twice about preparing for something which would take place only ten or fifteen minutes later, when she would be sitting in the first row, well-composed and ready to absorb whatever would be presented to her, among other children, who were pushing each other off the chairs onto the carpeted floor. She stood out among them: in her festive clothes, sitting perfectly still, as though in preparation for something big ready to happen.

Only now do we understand what a big role we had really played. And if we hadn't take such pains to show her those videos numerous times prior to taking her to the theatre, would she have acted differently? This is the question we still ask ourselves.

* * *

She sits in the first row, attentive in her cream khaki pants and white striped shirt we acquired during our last trip to Italy. (She loved her grandparents there so much, and especially the grass in front of their summer home in Montalcino, that, upon returning to the U.S., we often would find her in her room in the morning with a backpack loaded with Legos and other toys and with her favorite mouse and a bear in hand. Asked to explain what was going on, she would say that she had enough of the U.S. and was ready to return to Italy. As for us, we never could understand why she wanted to go abroad, since, in front of her, we never expressed our disappointment in the U.S. social structure and health care and especially education, something that to our European minds looked completely inappropriate here and in need of a major tune-up.)

So, she sits in the first row and we sit on the right, with the other parents, those vanilla-white professors and systems analysts, who immediately recognized us, the immigrants speaking in two different accents, and enquired, in their voices of steel and self-righteousness, whether we think that our daughter will be well-behaved during "Peter Pan." It was a group of theatre aficionados who always attended these performances with their kids.

For the first twenty-five minutes of the play she sits still, with us proudly ogling her from afar and admiring our late yet so beautiful child; we see how frightened she is when two actors, one in the costume of a pirate or a captain and another in the torn costume of a poor boy, jump into the audience and start fighting with their wooden swords next to her; she hides her head in her shoulders and covers her eyes, and we are almost ready to run toward her to shake off her fears.

Just minutes later a character named Peter Pan again appears on stage, in his green leotards and a funny, long hat similar to those that clowns wear in our countries; he looks so earnest, this young fair-skinned boy, that we are completely mesmerized when we hear him exclaiming, "Come! Come with me to Neverland!" He looks so convincing that we are totally enraptured by his words and wait in awe for his followers to run after him.

However, once he utters these words and waves his hand as though inviting others to join him, we see somebody small, in cream-colored clothes, climbing purposefully up onto the stage, crossing it and disappearing, after Peter Pan, into Neverland. With half the audience surprised and trying to figure out whether this performance is part of the planned action and with the other half of the audience laughing in crazy spasms and almost falling to the floor, we realize that it is our dear "Miss L."

She isn't sitting anymore in the first row—her seat is empty and none of the other children, who were fighting and shouting right before the performance, follow her. She disappears into a cutout in the wall, which apparently leads backstage, but we don't know whom to ask for an explanation.

She has jumped after Peter Pan to Neverland, and we, her parents, not familiar with this particular theatre and its rules, shy and hesitant to ask anybody for help because of our accents, sit frozen in our seats. The next act has already started, the lights have gone down and the show has started again, and we, the parents, with our late child away from us, with the seat in the first row without its expected occupant, with our hearts beating in panic, with our palms sweating, with other parents looking at us with strange sympathy or suspicion, we sit motionless in our seats not knowing how to react to all this and how to retrieve her from Neverland.

5

Boxes from Joseph Cornell

An old man reclined in a large folding chair, with drawers and boxes piled up at his feet. The scene resembled a lonely garage sale with goods spread right on the edge of the grass and no buyers in sight. The man's big head gave him a philosopher's look, and his deeply wrinkled forehead seemed monumental. Yet his thin neck and the white shirt with an open collar made him look boyish.

Protected from the sun by the shade of unkempt trees, he'd sit in front of his home for hours digging for something in boxes. Breaking for a moment, he'd grab miniature scissors and, with clumsy movements, would make perfect cutouts from magazines. For lunch, he would slowly yet steadily rise from his chair, straighten his back and go inside, to the kitchen, where he'd put his hand into a big cookie jar and get mismatched lollipops.

Returning to the shade of a maple tree with pockets full of sweets, he'd carry a sketchbook, in which he would draw and paste several cutouts. Then he'd sort miscellaneous objects in the boxes in front of his feet.

Suddenly a girl appeared on Utopia Parkway where he lived. She wore a short uniform skirt and her thick legs in scratched light-blue sandals were bruised in a sporty way; she was not chubby but sturdy and walked assuredly toward the old man. She was only eight; two teeth were amiss.

With caution, she eyed a large box she carried under her arm, as though watching over its inhabitants to prevent them from running away prematurely and scattering on the narrow road. Being a yard tall, the box made her bend to the side to balance its weight. She struggled not to drop it to the ground and, from her effort, was visibly red but tried to keep an "as usual" demeanor.

Inside the box, there were a starfish and several marbles, a whistle and a picture of a large cockatoo that was apparently trying to punch with his beak a little figurine of an ice skater standing next to him on a shelf. The box was quite heavy and the girl ran out of breath when placing the box in front of the old man:

"I brought it back!"

"Something's wrong with it?" the old man asked and put his head to one side as if he were a bird. He didn't scorn her but attempted to comprehend what had happened. What was the reason for rejecting his work? He didn't look at the girl but peered inside the box inspecting it and checking whether everything was in its place. He had the look of a weathered handy man rather than of a sensitive artist.

"I played with it and that's it!" the girl exclaimed. "And then I got bored with it, and I'd like to play with another. Can you give me something totally unlike this?"

The old man picked up the box from the grass and carried it inside; this was a work of art that would sell for half a million dollars at Sotheby's.

He came back with another box, made of wood of lighter complexion, but with a rich velvet lining, deep red. Inside there were silver stars and a ballerina's tutu, together with ballet shoes and delicate china. The girl looked with suspicion, rubbed her watery-blue eyes and smeared dirt on her nose. After she peered inside a glass door and saw the ballerina tutus in speckles of light and a starry blue sky, she took the box under her armpit, "Okay, this looks nice!"

Without bidding farewell, she disappeared at the end of Utopian Parkway, and the old man unwrapped a brightly colored candy, chewed it with a faint smile and continued picking things from a box filled with plastic doll's heads, legs, and torsos.

Joseph Cornell's boxes recall romantic nights spent in tacky motels, theater performances with distant worshipping of mysterious unapproachable ballerinas, cosmic scenes with hope for the existing eternity recreated with materials from thrift stores, arcades recreated with papier-mâché. I first saw a Joseph Cornell piece in the Peggy Guggenheim Museum in Venice, and forever remembered a long-haired doll, not a child but an invocation of a strange silent creature. Two or three years later, recognizing the illustrations in an art catalog, I remembered an otherworldly doll in a see-through box and finally associated it with the famous American surrealist.

He was lonely, lonely, lonely.

He was the only painter who cared about young kids.

A fine arts student once showed me her scrapbook with a newspaper photograph of an old, big-headed man with a large face. He bent down when talking to little kids who came to a library to see his collages and boxes. He carefully guided them toward his exhibition.

The show, which he organized only for children, took place on June 15, 1972, on my birthday and only half a year before Cornell's death. He made sure the art works hung at children's height. He talked to curators and asked them to remove the usual rope separating viewers from the art. He allowed his masterpieces be touched by little hands. He also served soft drinks and cookies to his little distinguished visitors.

I look inside his boxes in a museum: there are stars and hearts, marbles and pebbles, bubbles and balls. When I go to thrift stores to touch things to give tactile friends to my lonely hands, I see similar things: it's as though Joseph Cornell took somebody's memories from childhood and encased them into a box. Palm-sized dolls and beautiful buttons, cutouts of princely actors and actresses, old advertisements with fridges and cars and photos from time periods long gone. Those things bring some people back to their childhood where milestones were cherished objects.

In my country of birth, not only were the smell of grass and the postures of birch trees totally different (here, birch trees are stocky and stooped), but also the things we liked to play with. Cornell has no translucent red stars with the face of a curly leader we wore from the first to the third grade, or round, metal containers of shoe polish we used to push on the asphalt when jumping on one leg through squares drawn by chalk. I cannot find in his boxes those reflective sunglasses my parents brought from their Sochi vacation, or the collection of pins depicting Russian battleships with dream names, left after my aunt died in Khabarovsk in the Far East.

But his boxes remind me that in childhood we all had our favorite things which are now lurking somewhere in memory and can be brought up to the surface by art.

Cornell only removed an invisible rope and let us get closer.

6

MRS. FROST

Liz's *nyanya*, when we came to her small apartment in the Mission District favored by Mexican immigrants, invited us for an improvised tea ceremony and, upon seeing a plastic toy handed to her by one of the kids, a skinny doll in a white dress and with long silver hair, burst into memories.

"What wasn't I in Russia! First, I sang in a church and had to hide it from other Komsomol members. Then I applied to be a mailwoman and had to lift heavy bags with newspapers. This was right during the Perestroika, and publications were uncensored and a real pleasure to read, so I was saving some for myself and then would deliver them later. Third, I was a Snow Maid."

"Who?" asked Willy's father, a slender man, who looked quite "alternative" with his long hair, skateboarding shoes and a loose jersey torn on the sleeve.

"Snow Maid is a *snegurochka*..." the *nyanya* stumbled, searching for an appropriate English word and then happily finding it, "It's a spouse of Father Frost!"

"What? What?" Willy's father still could not understand and addressed his two-year-old son touching his knee, "Wait, Willy, I'm talking right now, be patient."

"She is also called Missis Claus,"—the *nyanya* responded, this time more self-assured, as though finding the appropriate English term for *snegurochka* was enough to explain her multi-faceted life in the former Soviet Union.

"If you are interested, I can tell you," said the *nyanya* and poured more tea into her visitors' large cups. "As an official Snow Maid, my mission was to deliver candies and toys. And since we delivered to all kind of kids and had to go sometimes to bad areas and climb dingy stairs with broken lamps, piss on the floor and no electricity, I was happy that Father Frost accompanied me. Yet, he caused problems!"

"Oh yes, he did!" the *nynya*'s husband added; he had no shoes, dark circles under his eyes, a scratched chin, and he had just come to the kitchen from another room where he had slept after his night shift as a security guard. "But my wife earned more than I did, me being a military officer at the time, during her trips! These jobs were quite lucrative, because Snow Maid and Father Frost would get gifts from the parents, like overflow of candies and wine."

The *nyanya* continued: "Yes, I would bring home bags and bags of chocolates when there were better times and would treat my parents and brothers with them. But when the bad economy struck, things became drastically different. Sometimes I would go to a store and buy the cheapest candies in bulk, so that children seeing me on the street walking through piles of snow in my uncomfortable Snow Maid suit wouldn't become angry and haunt me for not making them happy. They would surround me and pull my sleeves and look into my eyes, these totally hungry kids with only bread and sour cream available in our supermarkets. Those were children from the working class families whose parents were not only too poor to arrange a Snow Maid visit, but simply didn't care about their children and drank vodka instead of spending time with their offspring..."

"They were called latch kids!" the husband added,

seating himself on a small child's wooden chair and burying his head in his hands.

"So I would go with my bulk candies and Father Frost on my arm through these freezing cold Saint Petersburg streets, feeling as if my fingers were becoming ten icicles, and enter apartments. Everywhere were kids who expected more than their parents prepared for them. I would give them a toy car and they said they wanted a gun; I would give them a stuffed rabbit when they said they wanted a lotto game. And there was a line of bottles of every kind on a table..."

"Yes, spirits!" the *nyanya*'s husband raised his head, made a gesture at his neck as though snapping it with his fingers, and opened a little bar stocked with cognac and Stolichnaya.

Then he continued, "She would go with Father Frost and after a couple of visits like this Father Frost would get completely drunk"—the *nyanya*'s husband again snapped his fingers at his neck. "And then she would have to carry not only bags with toys for children, but also to help Father Frost to walk from one block to another, from one stair case to the next, in his huge red suit and felt boots. And his beard would get unfastened quite often, especially when he would drink! It's not easy to drink with a fake beard!"

"That's right," the *nyanya* said, "and soon Father Frost would not be able to walk. Then I would call the company I worked for and they would give me a fresh Father Frost, the one who hadn't a chance to drink yet.

And I would continue walking with him in the dark snowy streets delivering gifts."

"And this fresh Father Frost," *nyanya*'s husband added, pouring some vodka into an empty tea cup, "would get drunk too, since on each visit he would be offered vodka and spirits."

Again, the husband made the familiar gesture at his neck snapping his fingers. "You see," he continued, "in Russia it's considered impolite to decline. You would disrespect them if you would say that you don't want to join the celebration. And so this fresh Father Frost would get drunk after four or five visits, but they would continue going to sketchy apartments until they would give out all their gifts. With each time, Father Frost's nose would get redder and redder and soon he would not be able to move his felt boots… he would call a taxi and get a ride home."

"And I would continue with the third Father Frost!" the *nyanya* exclaimed.

Sensing that the story is finished, the husband poured more cognac into a tea cup and then found a flute glass in a cupboard and asked Willy's father, "Would you like some?"

"That's a good one!" Willy's father murmured and answered "Yes."

7

Chasing Ghosts

* * *

Among the sounds of kids playing and cups clinking, and the *nyanya*'s whistling teapot on the stove (which harmonized with a toy microwave emitting its final beep after Willy placed a toy bowl inside), a bell rang. At first nobody heard it, but it rang again, and the *nyanya*'s husband, in his bare feet, in several big jumps, like a leopard, covered the distance down the corridor and pressed a button on a scratched wall, managing to open a malfunctioning gate in front of the entrance.

Several futile buzzes later, after fumbling and fussing at the bottom of the stairs, a frumpy woman in a flowery dress finally entered the daycare. She looked like an English teacher and in fact she was one.

Nyanya, in her homey sweatpants and a ribbed rusty-colored t-shirt marred by woolly pellets (moments earlier she was trying to get a ball from under the couch and laid down on the fuzzy carpet) walked with a smile toward the newcomer. But the woman suddenly stumbled on a plastic castle and collapsed on the floor. *Nyanya*'s husband, accustomed to various little tasks around the house and not surprised anymore either by emptying a diaper pail or finishing up the bread crusts despised by the kids, rushed to pick her up and sit her on a chair.

She kept sliding back down onto the floor, and it became evident that the reason for the fall was not the plastic castle but a deep-seated problem within. Something was tearing this woman apart.

"Are you alright? What happened to you?" asked *nyanya* in her kindest voice, usually reserved for children's bruises and crying (in the former Soviet Union, *nyanya* was trained as a professional vocalist and mastered her voice's modulations), but the woman sat silently now.

"Her two children are going to attend my daycare in winter," announced *nyanya* to us. "They are very small and can't even sit up but in winter they should be ok."

"Not anymore!" whispered he frumpy woman, who was staring straight ahead, then looked around and saw cognac on the table. "I'm going to start drinking again; I became totally sober waiting for them, and now they are both gone!"

Nyanya's face became tragic like in a Greek theatre, and wrinkles showed on her forehead. It was obvious that she was empathetic.

The frumpy woman poured some cognac into a yellow tea cup that still had drops of strong black "Nikolai" Russian tea, but didn't drink. Rather she set it aside. "No, I shouldn't do this. My father died an alcoholic, and I should stop doing this to myself."

"Her father was a professor of political science," said *nyanya* proudly, as though showing that her daycare had only distinguished clients. "And her brother, when he was an intern, interviewed one of the vice-presidents."

Willy's father was trying to find the best moment to leave and finally thought it had come. He stood up, looked at his pants covered with bread crumbs, hesitated to wipe them away onto the clean floor of a day care, said bye to everybody and hastily left with his son.

Trying to keep everything light, *nyanya* introduced the frumpy woman to us, "This is Miss N., and she was planning to use my professional services."

I looked straight into the woman's eyes and saw the scene from fifteen years earlier: we are sitting on her bed, late at night, the lights are off, and we hear only murmurs of music pouring from her old CD player. The dark night covers us both, and only the green lights of the player and red digits of an electronic alarm accentuate our silence. Suddenly she asks what I had feared: if I can phone my work, take half a day off, and spend the whole morning with her.

Then, I was hesitant to say "no" to her.

Now, I was not prepared to confront ghosts from the faraway past.

In front of me, with her crystal clear blue eyes and straight blond hair, with the same rowdy tan which made her always look slightly drunk, since that's how her skin reacted to sun, sat my former lover Kathryn.

My husband was here and he knew nothing about my previous life and the women. In my daughter's mind, I only was in love with her *papa*.

Excusing myself, I left the day care in haste pulling my family with me.

At home, as soon as they went to the bedroom, I turned on my laptop and immediately found her blog.

* * *

"I am forty-three years old and a lesbian. After several miscarriages, I decided to find a surrogate mother, to finally realize my desire to become a Mom. When I posted my ad on a local infertility forum, I received an e-mail from Elimisha, who wrote that she would love to help people like me.

After legal and other arrangements were made, I started helping Elimisha with vitamins, advice on marital problems, and money. Several months later, a doctor confirmed she was pregnant with twins. Elimisha already had another child with a husband who was employed by the MUNI, and, in my mind, there was not even one doubt that something would go so wrong.

The closer the delivery date, the more jubilant I became.

Dives and one night stands were forgotten. Instead of six packs, my girlfriends would drop by with a crocheted blanket. At work, everybody was already informed and rooting for me. A card signed by my pupils and teachers was displayed on my table. Identical matching car seats had been bought and clothes for preemies prepared; I also decided on the twins' names. When on May 1st Elimisha and I came to a hospital, I felt nervous yet exhilarated: from this day my life as a Mom will start.

When we came to the hospital and Elimisha checked in and was scheduled for delivery that day, a midwife informed me that the Cesarean section would take twenty-four hours. I had to leave for a few moments to buy some produce. In a grocery store, I picked up a small lunch for myself and a large organic salad and frozen fruit bars for Elimisha, as I prepared to spend the whole night at the delivery room. I called her husband and informed him of this great news. However, when I came back to the hospital with my grocery bags, Elimisha was gone.

Surprised hospital staff hugged me and explained that she'd disappeared.

All calls to her place went unanswered; the next day, when I visited an apartment she had told me she rented, a stranger answered the door and said that she had never heard of anybody named "Elimisha." When I bitterly said that "somebody named Elimisha" had disappeared with my children Gerda and Kai, this woman suggested contacting the police to arrange an Amber alert to locate the missing children. But the missing children had not yet even been born!

Suddenly Elimisha replied to my e-mail and said that the delivery had been postponed. She explained that it was rescheduled in a different hospital. Gathering all my car seats and matching blankets, I rushed to this different hospital on the other side of the town, only to be confronted by hospital staff informing me that they "had never heard such a strange name."

Then the next e-mail came where Elimisha reported that she had gotten scared of the C-section and that she needed some emotional support at this point. Also, she said, her husband's union had finally authorized the MUNI strike and this strained her marriage and made her have pain in the lower back. I told Elimisha that everything would be fine and asked how my children Kai and Gerda were doing. Elimisha said nothing and instead gave me the address of yet another hospital where she was finally going to deliver my kids.

Yet when I arrived there, the same story was repeated: nobody knew about her there. E-mails stopped arriving. The MUNI driver, her husband, was missing, too, together with his voice on their home's answering machine. Strangely enough, the MUNI strike indeed took place in our city and finally ended with MUNI employees getting a raise. Still, at every place I would call or come, I was met with silence. No matter how hard I tried to locate the surrogate mother, she and my unborn twins were not to be found.

And what can I do now with all the things that I have arranged for these kids? Have any of you seen Elimisha? Please e-mail me ASAP with any advice. I don't want to press any charges, but I just want to hug my dearest kids. If you see them somewhere, just tell them somehow that I have arranged for them a beautiful room with blue and pink colored bassinets. I had already secured a place in a day care for them with a Russian nanny so that they could speak several languages right from their birth. I bought rattles and play mats for them and allocated a place in my heart for my children, only to be left alone with ghosts.

When a day passes, filled with routine walks, grading papers, and giving lectures to immigrant Laotian and Nigerian students whom I prepare for life in the U.S.; when I come back home and pick up a chilled bottle of wine; when I sit in a café stroking my pug whom I named "Tubby"; when I go to bed totally empty at night and feeling alone, my unborn children Gerda and Kai are always with me."

8

ON THE CAROUSEL

Elizabeth's mother sat with her daughter in a large red metal bear that looked like a gigantic cookie jar rather than a spinning and swindling device, and tried not to look at her daughter and husband. The 4-year old daughter and 44-year old husband were turning a crude metal table, which looked like a disk, in front of them to the right, and Elizabeth's mother knew that the bear was going to spin to the left. Elizabeth's daughter and father would continue to turn the metal disk in front of them to the right, and the bear would spin to the left—or at least this is what it seemed to be doing, but it was completing its tasks in such a violent manner that Elizabeth's mother only could grasp the metal disk with her cold sticky fingers and try to keep herself calm.

The bear guided by her daughter and husband was outdoing itself. The attendant apparently forgot to push the stop button and the torture continued for another five minutes. Elizabeth's mother always hated amusement devices and composed herself so as not to throw up. With this constant spinning and outside noise, she lost feeling for direction and time. She only came into these red metal innards to make her daughter happy.

The bear's innards were so dark that Elizabeth's mother could not see their faces, but she clearly heard loud laughter and joyous screams. With a cold forehead and the feeling that the universe itself was making her nauseous, Elizabeth's mother was resisting a desire to vomit and could not force herself to utter some words so that her family members would stop spinning the metal disk: this would have prevented the bear from jerking so violently.

Her husband and her daughter had asked her already five times whether she was ok, but she could not bring herself to say even a word. They asked again, "Mama, are you okay?" and even though she was not okay, she didn't answer. Like the bear itself, she turned into one big space filled with shaky organs all stuck together. The disk was turning to the left and the bear was spinning to the right now, and inside Elizabeth's mother everything went up and almost broke the surface, but she thought that it would be embarrassing to relieve her misery like this in front of other parents with their joyous kids.

When Elizabeth's mother was a child herself, she always vomited when a taxi was hired to take the whole family to their St. Petersburg suburb's dacha. Once she vomited in a trolley full of people, right onto her dressy wool pants, and she was embarrassed when passengers started asking each other, "Where does this awful smell come from?" She was eight-years old then and was going to a Soviet play about the Revolution, where a woman commissar was raped by a sailor and then thrown overboard during the revolt on the ship.

Now her nauseous, feverish state was becoming unbearable.

Deep in her heart, she knew that the red metal bear would never stop and would continue shaking and rolling in the dark, surrounded only by a few lights and the bright happiness on children's faces.

Elizabeth's mother thought that here, in this amusement park, near a freeway exit, in this park filled with its low-income inhabitants who exhibited a special love for cheap thrills, a child could be easily lost and nobody would pay any attention.

Just before entering the bear, Elizabeth's mother had watched her daughter riding in it again and again, relentlessly standing in line and then, as soon as the agent would open a gate, running to the red bear, always choosing him over other blue and yellow metal counterparts, and asking her parents to join her. Watching her from outside the gate, Elizabeth's mother fought an evil desire to disappear and leave her daughter here, inside the bear's metal innards, with her happy smile going in circles forever.

Elizabeth's parents would leave the park and go somewhere to relax and drink a beer after a hard week of work, and the daughter would spin with the other kids, not realizing that her parents were gone. Mad at the whole world for bringing her here, Elizabeth's mother was envisioning, with a vengeance, her daughter's face when she would realize how stupid she was focusing only on the spinning red bear and failing to notice that her parents were no longer with her.

Elizabeth's mother started envisioning other children riding in the metal bears without their parents forever, and suddenly the whole amusement park seemed to be full of these "orphaned" children oblivious of their parents' suffering and only minding their giggles and the mindless metallic spinning of hollow giants. Forcing herself to lift her head (now, after finally exiting the bear, she was sitting on the ground, with a strong desire to lie down right here, to prevent the earth from descending on her), Elizabeth's mother saw her daughter spinning in the bear again, and this constant spinning translated, in her mind, into eternity.

With a sudden burst of anger Elizabeth's mother thought that she could easily leave now, and her daughter would not notice her disappearance. When her daughter and husband finally disembarked from the large red bear, and the daughter asked her mother's permission to ride the bear again, Elizabeth's mother slowly slouched down on the dark dirty ground and closed her eyes. Then she did a slight gesture with her right hand, "Go! Go! You're killing me!" and swore in Russian.

Not hearing her, the daughter happily ran toward the bear together with her *papa*. Elizabeth's mother finally vomited.

In the late evening, after a month of protracted and sweaty attempts to conceive, her period came.

9

CARLSBAD CAVERNS

* * *

Two tall, large people with unidentifiable accents, dressed in red and blue Adidas t-shirts, as though members of opposing teams, were doing something to a small child who screamed in impeccable English that she was afraid.

Passersby in energetic sports pants and with flash lights, who cared enough to get a short glimpse at what was going on, were able to notice that these people had placed their hands on the child's head and were pushing it down as though handling a ball on a basketball court. The ball was resisting and was getting out of the basket, the basket in this particular situation being a two-toned (again red and blue) backpack carrier.

Concentrating on this increasingly difficult task (the screams of the child were getting more shrill with each push), the two tall, large people with two different accents kept up a short commentary on the event to each other, continuing to speak in two different languages. It seemed that they were able to understand each other's frustration perfectly, even without choosing adequate, mutually intelligible, international words.

They attempted to grab her flailing legs and arms, and guide them through the small openings on the two sides of the backpack carrier. The child kept screaming and, with a couple of frantic tugs, she again got out of the backpack carrier almost completely, so that the basketball game had to be started again. Meanwhile, tourists with flashlights, walking sticks and water canteens were energetically passing by without any hesitation and walking straight into the caves, not caring to stop and look at this natural wonder in awe.

A huge black opening in the earth stared at them in all its majesty, emitting a stale, yet not completely unpleasant smell of mustiness and natural mystery. This is precisely what the child was scared of: this all-consuming and hungry black hole which would swallow up her entire family once they moved in.

The child was born in Berkeley and, at four, had never seen any caverns; nor was she familiar with different weather conditions, so that when her family took her to "White Sands," a highly prized destination sought by tourists, with its icy-white sands almost blinding your eyes, the child felt so irritated by the awful heat that she kicked a white sandy hill with her toe, shouted, "I don't want to be in these stupid White Sands," and sat apprehensively right on the ground not willing to move even one inch. She ordered her parents to carry her to the car with air conditioning and the parents drove to Carlsbad Caverns where now they were struggling with her.

The whole trip, meant to show the natural wonders to Elizabeth, was a total disaster.

* * *

As soon as the two people with similarly big round faces and dissimilar accents started their descent down the steep route, built during the Great Depression to give hope and a living wage to state workers, the child stopped screaming. Holding her father's prominent head with her two little hands, she stared intently into the hole, now accentuated by punctured dances of miniature bats that looked like mysterious insects from afar. Their spiral trajectory reminded her of the movements of cut tea leaves in a cup, stirred by a spoon.

Inside, the two large people with accents and a whimpering child found grey stalagmites and stalactites, which a cowboy and explorer named Jim White called "hanging-downs" and "stickie-ups" and even "stickie-togethers", and people living at the end of the 19th century still didn't believe him when he emerged from the freshly discovered cavern with this news.

The child in the carrier backpack revived and even took several steps, touching grey stones, seeing in them "little bears," "dwarfs," "our little family with mama and papa" and even "a princess in her own room." Yet, when asked by her mother whether she would like to take a plane for the second time to New Mexico to explore the caverns, the child replied that she would happily take a plane but not to Carlsbad.

The child still insisted on flying to Italy "where there was a lot of green grass."

In the evening, at around 7 p.m., the same two people in red and blue shirts, speaking in different tongues, were seen in a specially installed "Bat Amphitheater" waiting for the bat flight. In front of their large feet in identical black nylon sneakers stood two bottles with water. One larger container, just taken out of the trunk of their car left under the hot New Mexico sun with no shade, contained very warm liquid; the small bottle was freshly filled with fountain water.

People sitting on the cement steps of the Bat Amphitheater briefly glanced at them and decided for themselves that the language this mother spoke to her child was German or French; as for the father, who seemed almost like a giant with his stooped, meaty shoulders, round calves and three-day stubble, he returned these unwanted glances with such a severity and displeasure on his face, that people sitting close to this family forgot about their linguistic diversity and averted their eyes. Later they decided that since he seemed to be speaking Italian, he probably was an immigrant from Rome (this was one of the two cities that came to their minds when thinking of Italy).

Suddenly everything quieted down and people, including the unevenly accented family, started looking at the "Bat Stage." It was announced by a park ranger in khaki pants and a hat that, after she shared with the audience a couple of facts about these creatures, the bats would appear in just a few moments.

On the Bat Stage, there was a large apparatus with one red and many green lights blinking on it. It emitted a soft clicking, and the audience who came to watch the "Bat Show" had been informed that the apparatus catches the bat's movements deep in the cave and when the clicking got a bit louder, everybody should stop talking and wait.

The small child, who succeeded in overturning a water canteen, clung to her angry Papa and said that she wanted to leave because she was afraid of whatever everybody was waiting to happen. Papa said he was looking forward to seeing the bat flight all his life, since the first time he saw the movie "Koyaanisqatsi," which depicted bats in all their multiplicity flying into the New Mexico sky. The child's mother, with her strong accent and rather severe and sharp facial features (she surely didn't have that wholesome American look), stared silently into the large and dark cavern entrance. The soft clicking, which emanated from the black apparatus on the stage, got a bit a louder, and then even more louder, and then it went with full force, clicking and squeaking.

One after another, dark spots started appearing from the bottom of the cavern and rising up; the clicking got so loud that it was almost unbearable, as though the apparatus with blinking green lights was begging for help. The ranger, looking very serious, turned off the machine and stepped back; it was still very hot but the evening darkness absorbed all the heat and left the impression of coolness.

In the total silence, right before the sunset, the small black creatures started chaotically flying in circles, from left to right and from right to left, seen against the background of the cave opening, and then emerging from the cavern and flying somewhere up and to the right, in an easterly direction.

One after another they would fly up and to the right, after their chaotic circling and whirling close to the cave's opening had been completed, and once the first ones had disappeared, the others would try to join them and lift up into the air and go up up up and disappear somewhere afar. Behind their chaotic swirling and then moving up up and beyond the horizon, out of view, there was a certain geometrical pattern or force which nobody wanted to decipher, relaxing comfortably on cement benches in a hot New Mexico night.

A large crowd of people, which gathered in a convenient amphitheatre built by humans under the open air, watched a large crowd of bats swirling up from the caves and flying up. With each new moment, a new batch of bats would appear from deep in the opening, perform its half-chaotic, half-geometrical dance and would go, one after another, into their determined flight and disappear into the night. When the last batches of the small creatures were still emerging from the darkened cave opening, people stood up, one after another, gathered their belongings and started slowly exiting the amphitheatre, one after another, up up the stairs and into the warm New Mexico night, in small trickles, exchanging small meaningless jokes, not waiting for the last bats and totally sure that they had already seen everything, unaware that somebody stared at them—*up up up and exit this life.*

10

THE CONSEQUENCES OF THE SAINT CARD

She came home without saying a word, dropped her yellow bag from her shoulder into the corner and lay on a purple couch staring up at the ceiling. The striped plush tiger Tatiana fell to the floor. He was still at home, finishing arranging sad, violet flowers, writing a "Get Well" card and inflating a cute Teddy balloon that immediately rose to the ceiling and ended up at the spot where she stared. She didn't blink.

He was almost out the door to deliver them to a retirement home and then to pick up their daughter from the Russian daycare in San Francisco. Holding a heavy vase in his hands, with water dripping on the flowers as if it were tears, he noticed that his wife had already come home from work, was lying on the couch and didn't move. "Hi!" said he suggestively, but she didn't look back, so that he was facing only Tatiana. He noticed that the plush tiger had immensely nostalgic blue eyes. "What's the matter with you?" asked he with impatience and concern in his voice. Nobody answered and he felt uneasy.

"I have to make it on time," said he, trying to balance himself on his feet, exhausted after spending the whole day at a designer table arranging flowers. She continued staring into the ceiling. He attempted to get closer, but stumbled on a hard hat their daughter wore when flying a cosmic ship with the tiger. Angered, he noticed a large crack running through the hat after he stepped on it. He felt a hot flash, as though his eyes and forehead were covered by a heated mask.

Yet, he still tried to show concern. "Are you OK? Sorry, I really have to run to deliver flowers to an old man! And I can't be late; the sender told me that he was taking his last breaths!" She said quietly as though dying herself, "Read what I just sent you online!" He put the vase next to the printer and didn't notice that the flowers, refreshed with MiracleGro, spilled some water on the paper.

"What happened? Are you alright?" he asked repetitively and raised his hands into the air, "What can I do? I have no time to browse through stupid articles!" She didn't answer and he pleaded, picking up Tatiana from the floor and placing her next to his wife on the couch, "Please, smile, tell me that you are ok!" She turned away from him, pushing Tatiana, and the tiger again ended up on the floor, next to the destroyed hard hat.

He looked at these toys and something suddenly clicked in his mind. "You know that I have to pick up Liz after the delivery to the retirement home? I have to go!" Again, he felt a sort of red heat around his eyes, as though his head was exploding.

"You don't have to rush!" she answered slowly. "It's very important for me that you read first what I wrote at work and e-mailed you. Turn on your Mac." She said all the words in a neutral voice, almost metallic, without even a shade of an emotion.

"It's very important for me, so you'll understand," she whispered almost with exasperation, and he finally jumped to the computer. While he was reading, she lay on the couch overcome by the sense of accomplishment:

now, once he reads this, he will understand. The "Get Well" balloon clung motionlessly to the white ceiling and the sun was setting. It was 6:30 p.m.

He had read an e-mail sent from her e-mail address to his rapidly and swore briefly, "What is this? Who cares about a Mexican saint from the 1920s? What a crap did you write?!" She continued starting into the ceiling with unspeakable grief and then slowly said, "Read attentively, I simply cannot say what happened with words; you have to read it. Then you will really understand how shaken I am."

He stared at the screen once again, trying to concentrate on this or that line, and then screamed, "It says that something happened to a 4-year old child! And that she was run over by a car! Did something happen to Liz? Tell me! Tell me right now! Did something happen to Liz?!" He jumped toward her as though he wanted to grab her, but she totally ignored this jump and kept staring into the purple material in front of herself. There was a faint white spot on the purple and she thought that there was no point to wash it off. Who cares, in light of what had just happened?

He did not know what to do next. She was the only holder of information about Liz, and she surely didn't want to tell him something awful, something really terrible, heightening his anticipation as in a theatre, intensifying the tragedy. He hated her at this moment: this "artist," this "writer," somebody for whom literature always superseded real life.

If Liz was in danger and a car had hit her, the truth had to be unloaded right away, without hesitation. They had to rush to the hospital and make her happy again. "Did something happen to Liz?" shouted he at the top of his lungs, but neither the "Get Well" balloon nor his wife moved.

She didn't understand what all this had to do with Liz. Is he OK? He cannot understand a simple parable? He cannot read? She simply wanted to relay all the mysteriousness of the day's event and how she was extremely close to death and how she was saved by the saint card of Toribio Romo she found. She wanted to show the exceptionality of her shock and even grief over this strange timing and coincidence; to bring to the surface all the inner workings of her life usually invisible to a commoner's eye; to demonstrate her refined state that allowed her to process these near-tragic events with literary skill and a well-sculptured elegance, and with unbeatable resourcefulness and resilience to her fate.

She was still surprised that the car hadn't hit her and that she was spared, and she wanted to share her triumph with her mate. Instead she was met with profound misunderstanding, with the gross negligence of his misinterpretation of her literary output and the murderous outcome almost caused by a run-away car. It dawned on her that for some inexplicable reason this big bully of a man with such fragile feelings toward their young daughter thought that this near-death experience had involved their little Liz with her thin limbs and high-pitched voice, so unnoticeable in the street that her parents purposely dressed her in orange, red, and other bright colors.

But while she was so acute toward her own fate that let her live longer, why was her husband so clueless toward her writing, toward the almost documentary "Saint Card"? Why wouldn't he ask her to open her maroon wallet and show her this talisman, this image of Saint Toribio Romo she now decided to carry with her from now on? How could he not understand that despite being rooted in real life, the story contained fictional characters and no children and animals had been harmed in the creative process?

She grew mute and closed her eyes.

"I will never forgive you if you told me a lie! You can't imagine how much I love Liz and I cannot let something happen to her! All your insane scheming! You live in your own head!" shouted he running down the stairs with a bouquet which was dripping water. "Liz, Liz, it's always Liz, as though I don't exist," thought she to herself and her eyes filled with tears. This was the moment she needed a hug to forget about the scary event, but he was out. She heard the door slam. All this was a huge misunderstanding that she hadn't intended to cause with her text.

She continued lying on the couch, staring into the ceiling: the only thing she needed today was some support but this was not given; moreover, her detailed descriptions of her inner world were misunderstood and discarded, causing even more chaos and pain. When she was a child, her mother would help by entering a room totally oblivious of her daughter's daily fights with the whole world, but with a large plate of washed fruits. Now her mother was in a grave and could not use a knife to peel the skin from the apples. The big truth suddenly dawned on her: there was nobody with a plate of strawberries arranged just for her; now she was herself an adult, totally lost in deciphering the signs and symbols of life; yet, even though she barely kept her head above the relentlessly moving mechanisms of the daily grind, and had no clue who was pushing the buttons somewhere above, she still had to offer protection to others. She realized that since she had grown up, there was nobody who could simply take her and give her a hug; and from now on there would always be somebody else's slim and small body needing protection; there would always be multiple children taking attention away from adults.

A Sauce Stealer

Someone whistled behind me. Then shouted thick, short words that mixed with the improvised noise of O'Connell Street. I didn't pause, imagining that I had already walked quite far away from the point where my fingers had gotten in touch with the ludicrously limp, laughably little bags, which I still held in my hands. Now I wanted to be left alone with them, in the sunny midst of it all. In the messy ensemble of strangers. In this melting pot of potholes, pints, and paddy wagons... Trusting tourists and thieves. Trams and trad Irish music pouring like beer from pubs. 'Be aware of pickpockets,' said a sign in the Ilac library that I frequented for free Internet, to send e-mails to Arinushka, my 10-year old daughter in Russia. But I wasn't a pickpocket.

I was a sauce stealer. After grabbing what I could grab, I got down the steps of a fast food fortress, enveloped by the determination of hunger. Firmly clutching my loot. Not letting it go despite all the arrhythmic shouts disturbing an even rhythm of the street. Despite the aggressive attention. 'We serve food 7 days,' the kind and caring sign outside claimed. Someone once told me that the eatery was located in an old bank damaged by shells from HMS Helga during the Rising. I passed it so many times on the way to my busking spot on Henry Street, where I sung my main course, 'Kalinka-Malinka,' sometimes side-dished by the accompaniment of an accordion, that it made me feel welcome. Did this pub just put a robe of respectability on its greasy, greedy fried shoulders?

A busy road at its footsteps. A Luas line. Pedestrians wait until a tram starts its movement—and rush to cross the road in front of it, like in a funny cartoon. An ATM where I used to stand behind people, just to glimpse their leftover balances. 80, 100, rarely 300 euros of savings. A pharmacy with a security guard watching that nobody appropriates long-winged 'Always.' A clerk who refused to sell me eye drops without prescription, leaving me with closed eyes covered with sticky and gooey secretions, as though I didn't want to face this damned world.

A tram line makes my head dizzy. I look left and right, not at all used to Dublin's 'left-handedness' after forty years in Russia. Under my arm there is discounted soda bread from an always packed Parnell Street Aldi. This time I examined it carefully—last week it was covered in blotchy green spots. Nothing to do with Leprechauns. It was banal mold. In a nearby Lidl, from the bread-cutting machine, it's possible to fish out slices left there by customers. Some of them drop to the floor. I pick them up anyway. Then dip a hand into plastic bins with salted nuts. When some of them are open, it's easier to dive in quite speedily. Not to be noticed. Cashews. Almonds. One needs to crush them with the teeth right away so that there isn't any evidence in the pockets. And if it's pistachios, leave the shells in the store. There are some already in one of the cartons with beer.

But sauces? I carry them openly. They are complimentary. They cost nothing, they're small.

Another shout from behind, now more determined than ever. But I don't stop. A hand touches my shoulder. A threatening closeness.

I didn't bother to hide the sachets, even though I could while walking away. But decided not to, for the fear of making a scene, for the shame of being searched. I carry the pouches without concealing. Together with the bread for 45 cents and a can of beans for 23. When you wash them with cold water, there is a white foam. The foam similar to the one that forms at the mouth of the crazy guy who cozies himself up in a sleeping bag near a tall office building on George's Quay.

I know that between 'Kalinka-Malinka' and 'The Rocky Road to Dublin' I could pull up a metal ring and eagerly gorge on the beans. If they were not from Lidl but from Aldi, I'd need a can opener but the vintage tool that looks like the Soviet hammer and sickle is in my attic. It's a tiny shivering space, a sort of Siberia, that I rent from a Latvian landlady on the dole, who used to administer illegal abortions at home. She gave all these Polish and Thai women a pill and then watched that they didn't die. A Lithuanian neighbor ratted her to the police, to make sure he is on good terms with the immigration. She spent a night in a jail and was released.

When she thinks I waste her resources—forget to turn off the light, dry the utensils or misuse a washing machine, she puts signs in four languages on my door which leads to the attic. 'Ne zabud vykliuchit' svet.'[3] 'In a kettle, boil only the amount of water you need for your cup.' 'Ná bain úsáid as an meaisín níocháin níos mó ná uair amháin sa seachtain. Má ta uait eadaigh a trimigh, úsáid on Radaitheoir.'[4] 'Noslaukiet savas karotes un dakši⊠as ar dvieli.'[5] Sometimes I'd like to use the rusty but sharp-tipped can opener I brought from Russia on her puffy face.

'Give me back all that sauce,' the Irish lad says. He finally caught up with me after following me for quite a while. His blue eyes are unblinking, his shoes pointy and spotless.

A young guy half my age, in a crisp white shirt with a red bow, with a perfect crew cut. His hair is the color of wheat.

I thought it was a done deal. That I got away. That nobody spotted me when I entered a dark hall and approached one of the tables. But I was prematurely happy with my petty gain in this big, powerful city of Oracle, Google and hopes.

Maybe I didn't pull those two tomato sauce packets fast enough out of the ceramic container, to have a

---

3   Don't forget to turn off the lights (Rus.)
4   Don't use a washing machine more than once per week, dry your clothes on the radiator (Irish).
5   Dry spoons and forks with the towel (Latvian).

proper meal this evening: this sauce, my bread and my beans. A packet with mayo was almost glued to my fingers but I didn't want to be greedy. I only craved a little extra to spice today's supper. Something in this bustling place full of office workers and wandering foreigners. The emerging energy of the enigmatic gem of a city that BBC recently called "The Second Silicon Valley". The place where Facebook and Pfizer could enjoy the 'appealing corporate tax rate of 12.5%.'

Today the sun shone brightly in the very centre of Dublin, right next to the General Post Office where the famous Rising took place. The post office from which a week ago I sent a cream dress, purchased at the Vincent's charity shop on George's Street, to my daughter in St. Petersburg. Near this post office a busker from Poland, thirsty from singing, ran after a cart on wheels with hot coffee, but was reprimanded. 'This is for the homeless.' She wasn't homeless—she shared a room with three Brazilian dancers. And sometimes a Hungarian tightrope walker joined them at night.

In the evening, beside the GPO wall, charity workers set up tables. Others sort through unappealing clothes, eat unappetizing food. One hundred years after the Rising. Glowing purple skin on the bare leg of an invalid beggar, showing wounds. An Irish acquaintance notices as a matter of fact, 'I thought they already halted all celebrations. But first they re-enacted the funeral of the Irish Fenian leader and paid tribute to the Rising itself, and then, when we thought it was over, they continued with commemorating the executions.'

The day before yesterday I was very lucky. The credit card machine at 'Kokoro' broke. Customers stood with their sushi, plastic containers in hand, waiting for the chosen hour when it would be half-price. I mixed with the crowd. Picked up a coin in a corner. Russian folk wisdom claims that when you pick up pennies, you pick up somebody's pain. Somebody's fickle ill fate. Ten cents forgotten in a ticket machine at Tara Station. A penny by a bird's feather, on the Rosie Hackett Bridge. Two pennies at the entrance to Spar. An hour more— and I'll have enough for my regular can.

There was a double paper bag with leftovers of edamame left on a table in 'Kokoro.' I took the cleaner one, put my sushi container inside. Purposefully strolled through the crowd. Quickly mixed with the improvised ensemble of people. Walked towards 'The Grand Social Pub' where jazz jammers sometimes leave their pints unattended on tables. Walked towards a bus stop and disappeared in the distance. Under the roof of the bus stop near the Liffey, quickly ate everything.

Escaping the barbaric and backwards Putin regime, I want to be Irish!

Stared at emaciated bronze skeletons in the Dublin Docklands. Learnt about the Great Famine and *Phytophthora infestans.* Heard about the ruins near Rathfarnham where they caught Emmet, who took part in the Rising. Apparently, he frequented the area to make love to Sarah Curran, his girlfriend. She was disowned by her father after Emmet was hanged.

My fingers still grasp two packets of sauce that would go so well with my beans. I don't want to let them go. My dream about today's tasty dinner. Mixing all of this together in a bowl, having a proper meal under the sun.

The young guy firmly holds my shoulder in its leatherette jacket. Repeats, 'Give me back the two packets of sauce.' Looks into my face with a certain persistence that shows that he won't waver. He won't go back to his eatery with the reassuring sign 'Food served 7 days,' unless he brings the sauces back!

On Sunday I went to Marlay Park. Saw old-fashioned women sketching near the castle. Then meandered through the myriads of emerald parks. Flowers flourished in this fertile land. The freshly green grass looked well-manicured. At Pearse House, they re-enacted the Rising, surrounded by the solemn black-and-white portraits of the glorious dead. Sang the Irish anthem. Dropped tears of rain. Umbrellas. An ambulance. White-clad women with red crosses. Solders in historic green uniforms. The Rising again and again. A slam poet invited me to a feminist vaudeville called 'Eastrogen Rising' but I didn't go, not to turn something that important into a farce. At the farmer's market in Templeogue, they would stare at my half-Irish friend with suspicion, 'What accent is this? Are you from here?'

And with a wink 'forgive' her half-Englishness.

Over the weekend, I visited the Pearse Museum's

café. Put a pack of brown sugar into my pocket. Then drank some cream from a saucer next to the counter. A rumpled woman approached me with a historical booklet in her hand. 'This is about the Rising. Only four euros.' I had no money. Could I sing a patriotic song to her, in exchange for the book? The soldiers who took part in the reincarnation of the Rising stood in line for their crumbled apple pies for 6.50 that I couldn't afford. Later I checked if anything was left on their plates. Just some lettuce with holes in it. The bullet holes in the salad leaves.

My fingers let go a little, but didn't want to part with the sauce. I still believed I could keep it. The eatery was so popular with well-off tourists. Americans, Germans and French who didn't mind to pay a fiver for 'O'Hara's' or 'Smithwicks.' I had a gaunt face, I didn't look plump. I didn't eat anything until this evening. Why was it so important for this young Irish man to put the tomato sauce back into its original place, into its square container?

My fingers still held two tiny packets of ketchup.

He said, 'I'll call the Gardai.'

And at this point, I had to part with my red sauce, and with it went my Emerald dream.

Pedro's Death Penalty

If only the California family law were fricking fair, the illiterate bastard wouldn't threaten my sis with the alimony she'd owe him after they finalize the divorce... If only she were less gullible and not a "stand-by-your-man" kind of gal, who hadn't glimpsed into this indolent idiot's credit report, therefore letting his debt balloon to debilitating proportions... If only she didn't give in to his almost illicit ploy and pleadings for a marriage, shortly before this intrigant had to be deported to Mexico... if only she didn't think herself strong enough to manage this monster with her own means, deciding not to involve her siblings and mother... if only the police officers hadn't been dispatched to a daylight shooting on Foothill Blvd., an afternoon robbery on McArthur, an evening disturbance and fireworks near Park Street, a sunset sideshow in the parking lot of a bowling alley that's on San Pablo... a mid-day petty theft at an ARCO gas station on the border of Oakland and San Leandro... an early morning bomb threat at a high school in Elmhurst (which tended to become frequent during the time of exams)... a sunlit bus stop in middle-class Rockridge where an erratically behaving teenager had grabbed a purse from an old classy lady, knocking her down together with her groceries (grapes and grains on the pavement)... or a place near the Planetarium where somebody saw a perv in black sweatpants and dirty-white sports shoes, luring mini-skirted schoolgirls into his grey pickup truck, when my sister came to their headquarters to file the report...

But before her futile, Kafkaesque attempt to file the report, before he had attacked her, flew off the handle and blurted out what he had been hiding for years, she already had an inkling that something wasn't right... read how to spot a psychopath in disguise... about the types of abuse, co-dependency and unmotivated antisocial personalities refusing to find a solid source of income for years... got soaked in sour forums about soaring love and low betrayals... buried herself in the colossus of comments... courtly remarks... canned responses and feelings and care-free rants... studied statistics, learning that she is safest when she doesn't threaten to leave, but is in extreme danger right when she makes her wish and her will well-known to her tormentor... learned the phrases "protective order," "money for relocation," "a getaway bag with documents and extra cash," "don't confront him directly but prepare to escape when things get heated up," and then went, with a pile of printouts from the Internet, to her best friend for advice... Still composed, still with perfectly cut, very short hair that he disliked and asked her to let it grow out, still well put-together in her immaculate clothes, but inside all falling apart... The friend could only hug her and pass her on to an organization for women... where these women—of all shapes, prior histories, hysterectomies, and denominations—hugged her as well.

They showered her with cheerful blue, pink, and yellow pamphlets, which matched their bright blouses and an open-armed disposition toward life (that's what they became after they ran away from abuse—self-assured and ready for everything except for taking anymore crap), and they embraced her with their well-meaningness and motherly moans...

She studied the pamphlets—apparently, while sitting on her queen bed upstairs in a little pink room adjacent to the children's room, where she had hung a poster of Christo with a date on it: "1963". It was a Vespa scooter wrapped in a pale-colored sheet, which, depending on the time of the day and her mood, looked to her—it called to mind a body enveloped in a piece of a translucent fabric—in her words, "either very erotic or very ominous"... She'd sit in the room, which, Pedro said, she'll never leave until the girls turn twenty one and circled two phone numbers... then crossed out the other, deciding to give her strength to just one... because she hadn't had much strength left after a dozen of years of this conjoined, coerced co-habitation, marred by his mumbling excuses about the money and occasional fits of madness during the fights... The circled number was the phone of the State Bar of California... which, in its turn, referred her to a local attorney, propelling things to start moving much faster...

In the office of a dry, dandyish attorney, who had two gold rings, one on the left, one on the right hand,

and two pictures of two similarly looking females on his desk, possibly of a wife and a late wife (we went to his office afterwards and he told us all he could remember of her panicked, panting visit), she learned that

—according to the California law, if the couple had accumulated a debt, it would have to be split between them in half, as well as their savings and assets;

—that she was not alone in this and it's better to finally attain freedom and suffer financial losses than try to change the person she'd known for years as a parasite, procrastinator, and ne'er do well;

—that this dry, dandyish attorney with yellowish hair and a bright yellow tie had helped hundreds of women in his twenty something years career, and their cases were all settled and they settled down and were happy, except for one who had ended her life right before the court hearing, messing up all the preparations and basically wasting everybody's precious time, but apparently this life-changing event was not related to her divorce but to a long-lingering depression and illness, either Lupus or Crohn or possibly a sickle cell trait that she had inherited from her Sicilian father;

—that despite Pedro's threats to take away kids, her kids most likely would stay with their mother—with her—because she does not drink, does not do drugs, is not promiscuous, does not leave youngsters in a locked car on a hot day outside a grocery store and holds a steady job, and even if her spouse tries to portray her in a drastically different light, with a barricade of wine bottles and bras torn in passion under the bed, her friends and neighbors will come to the rescue with their paradise-perfect and picture-perfect portrayals;

—that the court wouldn't award him full custody, as he very much wishes, in exchange for the house (whose mortgage is very much underwater due to the current economy), because this is not an appropriate trade or exchange, and especially because in twelve years of marriage he had never had a meaningful job, except standing on the corner in Oakland;

—that his first consultation is free, but the next ones will require an investment, which she can pay in installments, either with a credit card or a personal check addressed to "A. Krause LLC" but which will be worth it to her because she'll have the dollars and daughters all sorted out, and "A. Krause LLC" will monitor her each step in court;

—and that finally, at the end of their meeting, he'll give her a bonus, free advice, with no strings and no obligations attached... and that if she hadn't gained anything from their meeting except breaking into tears once when she said they had no money for fruits but Pedro always ate berries prepared for the children... so, even if she gained totally nothing from their one-hour conversation today, she still got this one useful instruction that will help to restore her composure, organize thoughts and evidence of his bad conduct and later present them in court.

To start a diary!

That's what he simply advised her: to go to a Walway or Savemart and buy a plain ruled notebook where she could jot down everything that was taking place in their house... jot down regularly... write down all episodes and events, in every detail, after her husband threatened to hurt her if she filed for a divorce and took away their kids.

The diary started:
February 18, 2015

I asked Pedro to assemble a metal bunk bed donated by a neighbor to our children. Seven months passed. My pleas, his immersion into the Mexico—Brazil soccer game on his immaculately new and well-cared for Mac, my constant reminders and his constant "yes, sure"... the bed stayed disassembled where it was. In the garage, for a very long time.

Finally, I brought down a well-used and well-pissed on mattress from one of our daughters' twin beds and deposited it at the front door. No pity for this material loss, even though usually I throw out nothing—since it had been discarded by previous owners at least two or three times. Now we wouldn't be able to quickly exit in case of any calamity like an earthquake or fire.

Pulled it down the narrow stairs, hitting on the way down, with the mattress' corners, the wedding pictures that hung on the wall. None of them fell, they just lost their balance and I evened them out. Pedro sighed, went at night in his beaten up pickup truck with a cracked windshield to "an undisclosed location" and abandoned it there. He knew several remote locations like this and in the past would break furniture—thrift store-style tables or war-times wardrobes—with his bare hands in a garage and then go, under a moonlight, to some place in Oakland Hills to discard the useless junk. All this not to pay disposal fees. Once he told me that he could commit a perfect murder and nobody would be able to catch him, that's how highly he thought about his knowledge of surrounding areas to get rid of the corpse.

The next day Pedro was on all fours for at least forty minutes, methodically assembling the metal bunk bed. As soon as he was done, our older daughter climbed up with her book, either "39 Clues" or "Warriors," and, after this ascent, we never saw her again: she was up there, with her head in the clouds, with her hands in her hair, rolling her locks over her finger while reading, at her age already thinking of becoming a writer and composing fanfic.

The younger one loved her "princess bed," as she called it, from the first moment: she loved everything princess, tiaras and silver stilettos, mellow-voiced unicorns, dancing elves, glitter and pink. In preparation for the assemblage of the new bed, my mother purchased the bedding: to get it perfect, she went to Anna's Linens multiple times.

The first time she discussed her options with sales

clerks, in her animated and energetic English with a robust Romanian accent, and picked up what they advised her to buy; the second time—after losing confidence that she had purchased the right size that would fit a new mattress. King, Queen, Twin—all these concepts were even more foreign to her than "King Pedro," as she called him, who, unlike men in Romania, was relying financially on her daughter and not earning much on his corner, where he waited for this or that landlord to pick him up...

"He should at least get a driver job; didn't he boast once that he knows roads better than police officers and could escape from them if in a chase?" she often would tell me but she would never say it to Pedro. He was fleshy, full-figured, fierce, and even my usually fearless mother was overwhelmed by his size. But for the size of the mattress... she was totally lost between King and "California King," and, after a conversation with me on the phone about how the bed looked and when Pedro was going to put it together, she went to Anna's Linens again. The third time—to exchange the second princess set, for something less cute and not pink, namely, for fishes and shells, after learning that the sisters, a five-year old and ten-year old, liked everything opposite.

She put a lot of effort into this touching gift, my aging mother, who after the death of her difficult, but doting husband, whom she hardly could stand, did everything to cheer herself up. She cut her hair once per month to look neat, added highlights to it, put a brooch from Latvia on her blouse (a little insect inside a bright amber stone), and went to a ballet as she did only when she was a 16-years old girl. All to show to him, to the still irritating and eerie dead, that she could perfectly manage without his earthly presence.

But I need to finish this diary entry. It's already a bloated one, since I haven't written for ages and tried to squeeze into this one many prior events that led to these days. Now I have to run to pick up the girls from the school.

February 25, 2015

A month earlier I asked Pedro to leave our family bed.

A dozen years he had already spent in it, snoring, squirting and sneezing, with a red face and sweat on his upper full lip, making both children on it, but never making the bed. Never putting an effort into vacuum cleaning or my vaginal orgasms. Never cutting his toenails, so that they looked sharp and scary like weapons. Another awkward habit of his was picking his elbows and putting a dry mixture of blood and skin into his mouth; during these moments I looked as far away as could... And looking far away into the past, before, he was never like this. When we just met, he wore size 36 and had no beavery beard; now he was pushing the size 44 and I could wrap his pants around my waist. And his thick and cracked heels... "I hate everything oily," he'd say when I would encourage him to put some cream on them. This would end any conversation about his personal hygiene.

When I was a little kid in Romania, my grandmother took me to a communal bath. Abundance of steam and of flesh. Soaps in hands. Sagging breasts. Enlarged brown nipples, the color of old leaves that were on the twigs of their sauna whisks. Fuzzy sponges and furry genitals between their legs. Camaraderie of bare skin. Of their full-figured bodies. The women did not shy away from the display of their flesh. I was a scared cute kindergartener, who did not know that in thirty-five years the same fat fate awaited me at every eukaryotic and prokaryotic cell's corner.

Now the skin on this former kindergartener's belly, stretched by two childbirths, is wrinkled. The womb is empty, unfilled. When she bends over her husband in a bed, she sees the folds of her own flesh hanging. Her skin is as ugly as a film of milky substance that rises to the surface in a pot after the milk boils. Here they are in the room with a huge marital bed… The man pulls his wife close, reaches for all the hot buttons at once instead of reaching them from afar… nipples, clitoris, anus, who cares… with no warning, no warming up, no foreplay. Just pulling and tugging and taking. After this he falls asleep very fast, washing himself and giving her a view of two enormous bellies. One in the mirror, another—in front of the sink. The still standing member is almost hidden by it. She looks at herself as though she is a different person... to distance herself from her own sagging shame and deformed defeat.

"I cannot breathe, careful."

"I know that you will like it. You liked it last time!"

"Please don't crush me. Move up a little bit. I'm suffocating."

"It can't be as bad as you describe."

My heart beats very heavily. When someone is having a heart attack, a slow pain spreads from the chest to the arm. My breast bone is crushed; between my legs there is a burning sensation. A smell of rubber, of lubricant, of his sperm. The heaviness on my chest is probably worse than angina. He weights twice as much as me. My heart pounds. 150 pounds for me and 300 for him. The math of our union does not compute. It's true that I never got into shape after getting out of the maternity ward. But the deformities of my body were caused by child labor, Pedro's—by laziness.

His mouth. A red full-lipped mouth framed by a thick bush of black hair, with its saliva showing between the teeth when he eats or when he hurls at me his disparaging comments. This contrast of red flesh and black hair, something hidden inside and covered by black brush, all this reminded me of female genitals. He looked at me, either shouting or pleading for love, and I saw a woman's pussy instead of his mouth and remembered those women in a Romanian sauna. It would be unnatural for me to kiss female private parts, so Pedro had no choice except to start sleeping on a dining room's couch.

It was perfectly equipped for sweet dreams. It was so apparent to me that since I am not inclined to be close to him, he should go elsewhere. Yet, as soon as he assembled the new bunk bed donated by a homey, heartfelt African-American housewife whose size was almost equal the size of the bed, he started sleeping in it. On the princess sheets. On ephemeral creatures from fairy tales. Crumpling girls' dreams. Smashing airy princesses in their cute castles. Covering the bright pink and bright gold of gowns and crowns with his pale skin with strange red spots in need of a dermatologist or a dietician since he literally ate all his sores. Pushing down magical wands. Obliterating the sparkles.

My younger daughter was crying.

Pedro continued sleeping on the princess sheets in her bed explaining that he had back problems from the old couch, and the more repeatedly I asked him to sleep elsewhere, the more repeatedly he would go into our daughters' room in the evening and lie in their bed, in the total darkness, with his computer. Only a bluish light on his Mac would indicate that he was there, that's how still and quiet he was, like an unmovable lizard.

In the beginning, our younger one came to him and tried to sleep in her princess bed on the side, because there was almost no place left for her by Papa's enormous body. She would peek inside, see the Mac and the blue lights, sigh and squeeze between him and the wall. I had to check on them every night, sneaking in, making sure she was not suffocated behind his hairy back, with her golden locks spread on the pillow with cheerful princesses. Occasionally she'd give up on reclaiming her bed and move into mine where I would read to her every night—whereas Pedro stubbornly stayed among the cotton castles and princesses.

My mother kept asking if the girls liked the bedding and if she should change it to a more appropriate size. She wanted a picture. She was old and she couldn't make it to our place; besides, Pedro was always in a conflict with her and didn't want to invite her to our family home.

"Snap a picture—how it looks with the children sleeping in it," she begged me but I had to explain that I could not take the pictures right now but that I would do it soon.

March 4, 2015

In the evening Pedro came home late and ate berries which had been washed and prepared for the girls. Blueberries, raspberries and boysenberries were very expensive, and many times I emphasized that these were for the children. For Pedro I usually left pears and apples but he would not even touch them, preferring pulled pork. Then he went right to the princess bed. I asked him again not to sleep there or at least to make the bed each day to show an example to the girls. He motioned me away, glued to his immaculate Mac. Then

I took out a camera.

The view was just horrid. Pedro was huge, with a bad haircut and grey hair, an immense unkempt man with a potbelly and thick legs, an overweight sea lion with a dirty mouth and fish breath, who used to suck all the life out and strangle beautiful princesses. Holding down their surreal thin bodies with his full weight.

I told him I'll show to my mother what he made of her gift. He asked me to go away. I took the first snapshot. He repeated that I should leave. As soon as the camera flashed in his face, he got enraged and jumped from the bed, asking me to disappear. I noticed that his thighs were joined in the middle and folds of fat kind of pushed into each other—that's how fat he had become. I took a second picture of him, in his stretched trunks, with yellowish spots in front from drops of urine, with a manly face distorted by anger. He took something out of his trousers' pocket.

Something flashed. There was a crackling sound, like firecrackers. Like it was July 4th instead of March 4th. Something black was pushed into my face. This was a Taser. The Taser he had showed me recently. He claimed he had acquired it for his late night walks from the parking lot to our house. He said he had only used it once during a dispute with a man who didn't want to pay him for installing his windows (Pedro actually came to this man's place a whole month afterward, during the night, and smashed all of them with a hammer wrapped in a towel, mad because of the nonpayment).

He advanced towards me. Pushed Taser buttons, enraged. It was a threat. I had to stay very calm to keep my composure.

"Don't do anything to me! Don't you dare move!" he screeched, as though everything was in reverse and it was me who was attacking him.

I had to come a bit closer to pick up my bra, in a dash to escape.

Moved a bit closer.

He put the Taser in front of him, in his outstretched hand. Shouted:

"If you touch me, I'll Taser you! Now! Stay away, bitch!"

"I'm only picking up my stuff and I'm leaving," I said very quietly, not to anger him more. Tried to be calm. Because the children were here. He was raging like mad. Standing on his toes, appearing even taller and bigger, and repetitively pushing the buttons on the Taser. Crackles. Light. Danger. The atmosphere was literally charged! I kept saying to myself and to him that I had to get away as soon as I could.

Something flew over my head and landed on the floor, falling apart. Two glass parts were lying within an inch of one another. In between there was a piece of a middle-sized carton. A picture taken during our wedding twelve years ago. Pedro, size 36, and me, size 8, with young full breasts, with unwrinkled smile and belly, in our best clothes. I was putting a ring on his finger. Now his finger was pressing a button on a Taser!

Our younger daughter rushed to the picture and picked it up. She held it close to her. Then kissed both of us in the picture.

"Don't do this while the children are here!"

Our younger daughter tried to put the photo back into the frame.

"You are a f*ing bitch!" he shouted. "Pinche Puta! You are a whore!

If you file for a divorce, you will see what will happen! You will be destroyed! You will not have even a cent in your name!"

He had said all these things before to me at least two or three times, but now, repeated and repeated again in front of our children, they sounded much more feasible, much more hostile. And I snapped too. Snapped both ways. Snapped the photo and simply "just snapped." Took a picture of him advancing at me, in his old underwear, with folds of flesh that should never be photographed and put on display, and announced that I would show his "manliness" to his mother, sending his picture to Mexico.

"You crossed a red line! F*cking cunt!" he shouted. "Do not touch my mother! Leave her alone. She is eighty already. Let her live her last years in peace without knowing what a bitch her daughter-in-law has become!"

"I'll send her a picture of you threatening me and I'll ask her to send me those eighty thousand dollars you are hiding from the American government in one of your

Tijuana accounts! And I'll live lavishly on this money with the kids, without fussing over each extra berry, choosing to buy only in bulk, just to save! I'll finally live a normal life! We earned this money together in the beginning of our marriage so at no point they should be staying in Mexico!"

And here is where he showed that he could not be a perfect murderer. That he was unsuitable for the role of an ideal killer.

Like Dostoevsky's Raskolnikov, who was so sure about himself that he'd never be found after killing the old female miser, he got too nervous, too agitated and he blurted out what he had hidden almost for the whole length of our marriage:

"You stupid cow! You think anything's left! All the money is gone! There is nothing in the bank account in Mexico! Moreover, I am in debt and now, according to the California law that I've researched, this debt is totally yours! Because I have nothing. I can't earn anything here without a degree! You were a fool to believe that my construction company brought me money—instead it ate all our savings... and even more... I'm drowning in debt. And you will pay it to the last penny if you file for a divorce! You earn the good money so you are doomed—you'll pay the alimony to me for the rest of your life! And I will take away the kids!"

The children were crying. I rushed out of the house and spent the night in a car outside a women's shelter. It had no space for me on that day.

March 6, 2015

I need to recap what had happened. To summarize for myself, to analyze and not to go crazy from raw emotions. When he was enraged, he told me he had squandered all the family savings and I was a fool to believe we still had anything left. I could not believe my poor ears. For years, he did not contribute; I was the major breadwinner and I counted on what we had hid in a bank account in Mexico.

Using my mobile phone, I retrieved the "Karma credit" website, pulled up his credit report and, on top of all things, discovered his $60,000 debt. AMEX—$1,182, CITI—$15,038, Barclays—$1,046, Chase—$17,297, Discover—$4,629, Bank of America—$20,000." All this shocked me: I always paid credit cards in full and shopped in discount grocery stores where all goods were marked with the word "FINAL."

And his confession was the last drop. It was that final straw that broke my back. The back of the mighty, motherly camel which was carrying the financial weight of our family for a dozen years. If before I hesitated to leave him or not, now his lies made our complete separation inevitable.

***

And this was the last entry in a thin, half-filled notebook, the last words that we have left of my beloved sis and that we'll use in court to press charges:

March 7, 2015

The next day after the confrontation I stretched my limbs (they were in pain from a chain of awkward positions I took during the night spent on the narrow back seat of my old "Mazda" hatchback) and walked to a police station in Emeryville. It was just several blocks away from where I parked. An early morning. Rare cars on the road. No people in sight. A deserted city. Everything's grey. The door to the station is shut very tightly. No entry. No way to get in. I call on the phone attached to the wall. The dispatcher answers and asks me if I had been hurt.

"Where were you attacked? Are you bleeding? Do you need help? "This happened at home." "Where exactly? In which location?" "In Oakland." "Then go to the Oakland police. It's on 7th and Broadway." "But I can't drive there, I feel like I'm gonna collapse," I answer him. And then explain, sounding reasonable: "I spent the night in the car because I was afraid to come home." "If it happened in Oakland, that's where you're ought to go," he sternly repeats. I hang up. Then, still at the entrance to the Emeryville police station, I ring the Oakland police. Shaking. Hardly standing on my feet, with my head flying above me like a balloon.

The dispatcher for the Oakland police does not take the report over the phone and orders me to come to the station in person. "Do you know where we are? We are on 7th and Broadway. Just come to the grey door on the side of the building and ring."

"Yes, but I'm not able to drive... I spent a sleepless night in the car because I was afraid he would attack me again. I am hurt."

He asks me familiar questions, "Are you injured? Bleeding? Did the attacker do something to you? Where is he right at this moment? Is he your husband?" I answer that I am ok and I would drive to Oakland myself.

Once I make it to Broadway, I park on an empty boulevard (it is early morning), go inside and ask at a bulletproof window where to file a report. A shabby building. Bare walls and memorial plaques here and there. A black woman at a window, a white man at a table. Another colored man walking down the stairs. So blurry. So burly. I ask one of them where I could file a family violence report concerning what had just happened to me. He asks me, "File what?" and dips a spoon into his yogurt cup. The flavor is blueberry. He dips the spoon into the cup and then into his mouth and stares at me. He is ready to swallow once he gets a response. I repeat, more clearly, "Family violence." The police officer with the yogurt consumes one more spoon and motions towards an old-fashioned black plastic phone attached to the wall, telling me to call the dispatcher. I call the dispatcher. This time I hear a different voice. I inform this voice that I had already called previously, about twenty minutes ago, and they instructed me to come to the station. "When did you call?" a female voice asks me quite sternly. "Twenty minutes ago. When I was in Emeryville trying to file a report there, in person. They told me to go to Oakland. And here I am." "What's your last name?" she demands more information from me. I tell her my name. "What's your address?" I give her the address. "Let me search for the record… No, I cannot find anything that you have told us. Are you sure you called this number today? Are you hurt? Can you go home and wait for the police?"

She repeats that she does not find any mention of my previous phone call in the police database. She instructs me again to go home and wait for the police. I object and mention that I spent the night outside, in a cold car, under the night sky, afraid to return home. "Is the person who hit you located in the residence?" she has to know. "Where is he right now?" she clarifies. I answer that I have no idea and that I'm afraid to go back home and wait there for the police. I would prefer to wait here, at the police station on Broadway, with this guy with a cup of yogurt and a spoon, with this black woman behind the bulletproof glass, in relative safety. I also would like to object that I never said someone had hit me, since he did not hit me but he attacked me with a Taser and I do not want to distort the events. I only want to file a report.

"Stay there and wait for a police officer," that's what she says. "How long should I wait?" I inquire. "Whatever it takes. The wait could be lengthy," this is her answer. "How long?" I would like to find out. "It could be long." "But how long? Hours? Days?" I try to keep calm. "It could be quite long," she sternly repeats. "Our officers are all on assignments, they are very busy today. This is East Oakland."

"OK, I will wait."

I start measuring steps. Back and forth. Back and forth. Past the white officer with the yogurt and spoon behind the clear bulletproof glass. Past the black woman behind another bulletproof glass. Looking at empty walls. At the grey speckled granite of the vestibule floor. At a list of fallen officers on a black plaque. They were killed by a guy who had ambushed them in an apartment they entered. I pace back and forth. The yogurt guy does not care. The black woman is overweight and she is occupied by her things. I'm waiting for the officer to come and take my report. The moment will come and the doors will open wide. I would look to see who is about to enter the building. Hopefully, a robust rookie from CHP. A man or a woman in a uniform. Someone in power. Someone willing to help me. Hopefully the door will finally open and it will not be my spouse looking for me. Coming here with the kids.

While I'm thinking this, the door suddenly opens and a stroller with a baby in it slowly enters, pushed by a man. This reminds me of my husband and how he pushed our daughter years ago. First one and then the other when they were growing up. Luckily, it is not him this time. What if he comes here to look for me now? Will he attempt to Taser me again and again, despite being at the police station? Once he smashed my iPad, just stepped on it and crushed it with his foot, when he didn't like how I was talking to him.

What if he indeed comes here to file a missing persons report?

My phone rings at this thought. It is my older sister. She says my husband was going to file a missing persons report but someone told him to wait, so he was not going to the police station right away but could appear here at any moment. I look at the door and I freeze in my tracks. A stroller is being pushed in and again the man who enters looks exactly like Pedro. Except that we sold a stroller like that on Craigslist years ago. Obviously it was not him, but I trembled a bit.

One more hour passes. No officer to take my report is in sight. I glance at the African-American woman behind the glass window. Sometimes she got out of her glass booth and walked to another room, possibly to stretch or have lunch. The burly officer is finishing his yogurt right at his desk. He had several cups of this blueberry yogurt and also an apple. In front of him there is a monitor with multiple windows that he peers into. The plaque with the already familiar names of three fallen officers is still on the wall and the officers are still dead. I pick up the receiver. I say I already called and nobody had come to take my report. They ask me for my name, for my last name and for my address and if I am ready to go home and wait for a police officer to arrive and take a report. "Go home and wait for the police there; our officers are on assignments, it could take a very long time."

I say that I am afraid to go home. "Is the person who hurt you located there right now? Do you know where he is? Is he your spouse? Are you physically hurt? Do you need help?" the voice keeps asking me again and again. "I have no way to know," I say thinking that at any minute he could come in and see me trying to file a report. "Your request is still pending," she says to me finally. "When will somebody arrive?" I repeat like a broken record. "I can't answer your question," she says. "I just told you your status is pending." "Will I have to wait at the station indefinitely?" I ask, losing patience. "We can't tell you, ma'am," she responds. I say that I'll wait for 24 hours until somebody comes, and then I hang up. Before hanging up, I emphasize that I'm still waiting—but not at home, I'm waiting and pacing and walking from one wall to the other, from one memorial plaque to another memorial plaque, at the police station on Broadway and 7th where they told me to come.

In two hours I approach the black plastic phone that hangs on the wall and call the same number. A different voice answers. I say I need to file a report. "What is your name?" I hear the question. I answer and mention that I've called before numerous times. The voice says she'll retrieve the entry about me. "What is your name again? Could you spell it for me?" she asks after a brief moment of silence. Then she adds: "There is nothing here. Did you call our number? Did you call from your cell phone or did you call from our phone on the wall?" She cites the number. "Yes, this is the number I called". "When did you call us and what did you say? What is your address?" "I've been waiting for hours,"—I start getting upset,—"and I plan to call every hour to see if an officer is coming."

"What's your address?" she asks. Finally she is able to find my file by the address. She says no officers are available yet but my status is "pending." "If you went back home, she says, and waited for us there, it would be much better." "I can't go home," I claim, "because my husband could be there at home and his past actions have convinced me that he is very dangerous. He attacked me with a Taser. I don't think it's legal. I'll be waiting here at the station. Will someone finally come?" "We have no way of knowing," was her reply. "Why?" I hear my own voice trembling. She nevertheless answers: "There've been a lot of shootings in East Oakland, so all our officers were dispatched there. International, Foothill, McArthur, Elmhurst—they are all there. And 98th. And something's happening close to the Coliseum." "I'll call in exactly an hour to check if someone is coming," I say. "Yes, feel free," the voice says and hangs up. "You can call us any time you want." The door opens and this time it is Pedro, without a stroller but with our daughters, who enters this government building. I see him before he sees me, because I lean on the faraway wall.

The children are with him and he is asking where he can file a missing persons report. "My wife disappeared," he says. "They told me to wait for at least for twenty hours before filing the report, so I waited a bit but now my patience is running out." They ask him to move to the next window to take some papers to fill out and this is when he notices me. And this is the story: I was at the Oakland Police Station waiting for an officer to report family violence—but, instead of the officer, my spouse who attacked me appeared. Because he truly worries about me. Because he cares immensely about my health. Because he knows all my thoughts and caters to all my desires. Because he is so sure I will stay forever with the family. Inseparable. Never apart. In a little pink room with a wrapped Vespa that looks like a lifeless body wrapped in a sheet. With a poster dated "1963," which is not only the year Christo wrapped the scooter, but also the year of Pedro's birth. I have to come home now, with the children. With him. Because of his unconditional love.

"We were worried about you. Come home with us," that's what he says proudly looking at the guy with the yogurt and the black woman occupied with her things. Here is his wife. Here are his young daughters. His major achievement.

The children embrace me. We go home together—

it is almost according to the scenario the voice in the receiver suggested to me—to go home and to wait for the police to come and take a report. And we go back to our home together... except that the police officer probably arrived late in the day after a shooting or theft assignment and left. Left because he didn't find me there waiting for him. I see in my mind how the officer looks at the empty yogurt cup and then at the plaque for the three fallen deputies, who are still very dead, and then at the black woman immersed in her things, and shrugs his broad shoulders. While I'm waiting and waiting and waiting for anybody to come to my home to take the report—sitting outside the girls' room, at night on the dark stairs, while my husband is sleeping inside in a princess bed.

March—October, 2015
San Francisco—Dublin

Margarita Meklina is a bilingual essayist and fiction writer born in Leningrad and currently residing in Dublin. An author of five books published in Moscow, she was awarded the Andrei Bely prize for her collection of short stories, *The Battle at St. Petersburg* (2003). In 2009, she was awarded the Russian Prize, established by the Fund of the First President of Russia Boris Yeltsin, for her manuscript *My Criminal Connection to Art*. Her English-language articles and fiction have appeared in *The First Class Lit*, *The Context* (Dalkey Archives), *The Cumberland River Review*, *The Quarterly Conversation*, *The Honest Ulsterman*, *Gorse*, *The Brooklyn Rail* and *Words Without Borders*. Her short stories in translation to English appeared in *Flash Fiction International* (W.W.Norton, 2015), *The Mad Hatters' Review*, *Reunion*, *The Toad Suck Review*, *Eleven Eleven* and many other publications. She co-authored the epistolary novel *God na pravo perepiski* with poet and essayist Arkadii Dragomoschenko and completed a young adult novel in English (*The Little Gaucho Who Loved Don Quixote*, 2016). She thinks, dreams, loves and writes in two languages.

www.ingramcontent.com/pod-product-compliance
Lightning Source LLC
Chambersburg PA
CBHW060549190726
48283CB00003B/939